AFTERCARE

INSTRUCTIONS

BONNIE PIPKIN

AFTERCARE

INSTRUCTIONS

FLATIRON
BOOKS
NEW YORK

AFTERCARE INSTRUCTIONS. Copyright © 2017 by Bonnie Pipkin. All rights reserved. Printed in the United States of America. For information, address Flatiron Books, 175 Fifth Avenue, New York, N.Y. 10010.

www.flatironbooks.com

Designed by Anna Gorovoy

The Library of Congress Cataloging-in-Publication Data is available upon request.

ISBN 978-1-250-11484-6 (hardcover)
ISBN 978-1-250-11483-9 (e-book)

Our books may be purchased in bulk for promotional, educational, or business use. Please contact your local bookseller or the Macmillan Corporate and Premium Sales Department at 1-800- 221-7945, extension 5442, or by e-mail at MacmillanSpecialMarkets@macmillan.com.

First Edition: June 2017

10 9 8 7 6 5 4 3 2 1

For Jesse and Peggy, my most amazing parents

AFTERCARE

INSTRUCTIONS

PREPARATION

A Few Things They Tell You:

- No food or drink for six hours prior to appointment time.
- If you receive the IV conscious sedation, make sure to secure a ride home or have an escort for public transportation.
- Dress in loose, comfortable clothing, with socks and flat shoes. Bring an extra pair of underwear and a sweater or sweatshirt.
- Bring picture identification and your insurance card

if you are planning to use insurance. Payment is collected in full at the time of the visit.

- One, and only one, escort may accompany you to the health center. Your escort will be asked to wait in the designated waiting room, and will not be allowed into the medical center with you.

The Thing I Wish I'd Known:

- *I love you* doesn't come with any guarantees.

CHOICES

Sometimes you make a choice that can save your life. You might make your choice for one reason, before the real reason even becomes clear. Like this morning when I refused the sedation. The reason was because I wanted to feel it. I wanted to feel my choice as it left my body. I didn't know it would actually make all the difference in the world when my one, and only one, escort bailed mid-procedure, and I found out by walking into the waiting room, scanning a sea of hopeful eyes, and finding absolutely nowhere safe or familiar to land. In that moment, I was thrown into the deep, deep water. And in the deep, deep water, there is no way to breathe.

Yet somehow, something propels you forward. Survival mode, I think it's called.

You can do this. Just get yourself to Port Authority. You've done this before, when Rose wanted to shop for stupid dance dresses in SoHo. You've done this when you've gone to visit Delilah. You can get yourself home. To get back, you have to move forward. Just move forward.

I cross the street and stop. Pull out my phone and find the screen black. Blank. I squeeze it like I could force out a text message from Peter. A text telling me he will be right back for me. That he just had to go get something real quick, some city errand he wanted to take the opportunity to do, and that he's so sorry it seemed any other way. And that he *loves me*. And that maybe one day we'll be ready, but we made the right choice for right now. And that he's here for me no matter what. No matter that our lives are so different, and no matter that I don't have anyone offering me guidance. That he's here for me while I figure this shit out.

But nothing appears.

And I have to figure out how to get myself home now. No sedation, no escort. Just me and my extra pair of underwear.

This is what echoes in my brain: *You don't have to do this, Genesis. There are other choices.*

But I push that away because he knows why I had to do this. I explained myself, didn't I? And anyway, the choice was for *us*, not *me*. I push and push our conversation back back back into the grayest part of my brain, and remember I'm standing on Bleecker and Mott in Manhattan, across from the Planned Parenthood. And there is a hole in the leather of my boot I'm wishing more than ever I'd actually taken to the cobbler to get patched.

Voices stretch across the concrete and the speeding taxi-cabs fuzz and buzz into each other. Three lonely protestors smoke cigarettes through fingerless gloves, with their signs propped against the building. It's a much different scene in Jersey. Which is partially why we came here this morning. More anonymous, I suppose. Easier to blend. No one to run into.

I watch a girl exit the building with her escort. She was in the recovery room with me. Where they sat us down and left us to bleed and ooze until we were ready to walk ourselves out. The girl and her escort have the same wild hair and deep-set eyes. This has to be her mother, and I try to imagine my own mother helping me out, escorting me. But I can't conjure the faintest image of this. Not anymore.

"Are you okay?"

She's standing right in front of me now. Do I look abandoned? Do I look lost? Do I look like I need help? I see my sock sticking out through my boot.

"I guess so."

"Where's your ride?"

I don't answer.

"Where are you headed?"

"New Jersey, I guess."

"Well, do you know your way?"

"I can figure it out. I'll be fine."

She wiggles out of her mom's hold, and steps closer to me. I stare hard into the ground, not really sure why I'm refusing her help.

"Here," she says. "Hold out your hands."

I do as instructed while she reaches into her saggy black bag. I see the vinyl peeling off in patches.

"I'm fine from here," I say.

"I know. I heard you. Just hold your horses."

My hands are still out like an idiot, while she digs and digs.

"Ah, there we go." And with that, she drops a handful of lollipops into my hands.

"They were free," she says with her mouth half turned. Her escort-mother shakes her head and smiles while I hold back tears burning in my eye sockets. I say thank you and keep my head down while they walk away.

Then I put my cousin's address into the map function on my phone. I don't think I'm far from her dorm. I should have had her meet me here in the first place. Or Rose. But how could I have known he'd just leave me?

I followed his conditions. I didn't tell anyone. Not a single person. Even when that broke me apart. Even when I started to feel sick, and started to bloat, and had to make up excuses to the people who would notice. I kept it inside. Held it tight. Like he wanted.

Directions:
14 min.
Route overview: 0.7 miles
Walk 0.5 miles, then take a right on Macdougal St.
Walk 0.2 miles, then arrive at the destination.

Sounds easy enough. No hidden turns. No secret passages. Just walk straight, turn once, and arrive. Those are the kind of instructions I can handle. If I have to think any more, I might just melt into a puddle and freeze into the cracks in the sidewalk.

The wind whips between buildings and slices into me as

I walk. I pass by the hole-in-the-wall falafel place where Del took me once before, and the smell of fried food and onions makes my stomach twirl. The line is out the door and down the street. Even in the dead of winter. Finally, I see the building on Washington Square Park with the purple NYU flag hanging like my beacon of light.

In the lobby of Delilah's dorm, a tired, grayish doorman in uniform with the name *Hunnigan* on his badge sits on a stool at a podium. He's doing a crossword puzzle and listening to low, bopping jazz music on the radio. He looks up when I approach, but doesn't say anything.

"I'm here to see Delilah Reese."

He plucks his glasses off and they drop to his belly, dangling by the string around his neck. "She has to sign you in."

He points to a sign behind his head telling me this very thing. Also telling me I have to leave my ID at the desk, and I'm once again thankful for today's preparation instructions. I set it down in front of him.

"She's got to come down, darlin'. I can't let no one up without a resident."

His words blur as my head lightens and my feet grow heavy. It's as if all my blood is spilling through me and down to the ground. The music sputters and spits. I grab his podium for balance.

"Are you okay?"

That question again. And how to answer it? I know I should not be alone right now. That I need someone.

I nod. And move to a seat on the window ledge.

I call Delilah, but it goes to her voice mail.

I'm about to drown in my stomach bile. Where is she?

Where is *he?*

I call him. Peter.

Voice mail.

But my voice doesn't come to me, so I hang up without leaving a message.

Then I call him again.

Voice mail.

Fuck. Fuck. Fuck. Did he just disappear? Did he leave this planet? Did he leave the Genesis and Peter planet we set up camp on and inhabited for a happy little while? Where we built our own atmosphere and were working on making a beautiful place? I liked our planet. Now I'm lost in space. No sound. No air.

I call him one more time. You know where it gets me. But as I'm listening to his outgoing message, the phone vibrates in my ear. A text.

Delilah: *What's up? In class. Can't answer.*

It makes me smile to imagine her sneaking a text message in some philosophy class or history of street poetry or wherever she might be.

Me: *At your dorm. I need you.*

Delilah: *Out in 10. Then 10 min walk. Can you wait that long?*

Me: *Yes.*

I think.

I've made it this far without collapsing. She doesn't ask me what's going on. If she did, I wouldn't know how to take this knot inside me and untangle it into words.

I curl up into the cushion and lean against the cold condensation on the window, tucking my knees up into my chest.

Two girls dressed alike in black-rimmed glasses and striped sweaters stop by the door to arm themselves up with winter layers. The shorter girl is louder than the other and she's talking about an audition. The other, with the static hair, is assuring her she did an amazing job, and she for sure has the part, and the loud girl is whining about how she's a total fraud and one day someone is going to realize.

Actors. Once upon a time I called myself an actor too.

The pair gets distracted by a boy in a brown hat with animal ears and rubber boots. The whining girl strokes his fake ears, and purrs into the real ones. Hunnigan asks them to move away from his podium.

I was in my first play when I was twelve. It was a big deal because I was the only kid in the show. Not that it was a big part or anything. I was in two dream-sequence scenes. The director was a real alcoholic maniac and the highlight of his career was when he was in an action-adventure movie with Jean-Claude Van Damme where he gets stabbed in the neck with a chicken bone. I don't know if I was actually supposed to watch that movie, but there have never been too many boundaries in my home. I guess that's why my dad let me be in this play, with a washed-up movie villain at a community theater downtown. No boundaries. Dad would take me to rehearsals and wait for me in a coffee shop down the street. He knew Brad, the director, probably from meetings, but didn't interfere. Didn't play the dad role. He was so proud, though. He really wanted one of his daughters to be into theater or art or music. His excitement would pulse whenever I'd get into the car after rehearsal. He'd hold back on asking me questions, but tap his fingers against the wheel, waiting for my report.

Anyway, this director was way into meditation. We'd warm up with a breathing exercise and half the cast would fall asleep, but I always liked turning my mind off. I haven't meditated since. And I stopped with the theater thing after my dad died. I couldn't imagine performing without his face in the audience.

I might feel like a fraud too.

Trying to remember the meditation techniques Brad gave us, I tell myself I am not in a steamed-up dormitory lobby. I am alone with my thoughts. No. No thoughts. I am on a mountaintop. All I hear is the steady and constant sound of wind.

Except on this mountaintop, I can't stop thinking about how I ended up here.

All the way up here.

And who is not here with me.

Exactly twenty minutes later, Delilah stands in front of me in the lobby. I hold on to her as she signs me in and takes me up in the elevator to the eighteenth floor. Without asking any questions, she tucks me into her bed and I fall asleep, black and dreamless.

Safe place.

Mind off.

ACT I
SCENE 1

(This scene takes place in the Morning
Thunder Café, a popular after-school
hangout.

At rise, two teenage girls can be seen
in a booth. The décor has a vague
fifties vibe. The girls are stylish in
an alternative kind of way. Not over
the top, but not mainstream. GENESIS has
a slightly darker vibe to her. ROSE has
a more sexual edge.)

GENESIS
Do you know Peter Sage?

> ROSE
>
> What do you mean? Of course, dummy. Everybody does.

> GENESIS
>
> Yeah, but, like, do you know him? Have you ever talked to him?

> ROSE
>
> What do you want to know about him?

> GENESIS
>
> Well, I mean, uhhhh . . .

> ROSE
>
> You mean, "uhhhh"?

> GENESIS
>
> Never mind. Forget it.

> ROSE
>
> What?

> GENESIS
>
> Okay, well, does he have a . . . girlfriend?

                    ROSE
          Peter Sage? With a
          girlfriend? You think his
          nutso religo-freak
          parents would let him
          even talk to a girl? Much
          less slip his hand up her
          blouse?

                    GENESIS
          He talks to girls.

                    ROSE
          Yeah, at Bible study.
          And that creepy morning
          prayer circle in front of
          the school.

                    GENESIS
          He's not in the prayer
          circle.

                    ROSE
     (Raising eyebrows)
          What? You looked?

                    GENESIS
          He's not like that. I
          mean, not like Mitch
          Jennings or Hannah and
          all those people.

                    ROSE
          Why are you paying such
          close attention, young
          lady? Does someone have a
          little crush?

                    GENESIS
          No! Come on. Get real.
          Peter doesn't like girls
          like me.

(SERVER dressed in a vintage waitress
dress drops off a mountain of cheese
fries and two Cokes. ROSE digs in.
GENESIS plays with her straw.)

                    ROSE
(With her mouth full of fries)
          Girls like you? You're the
          best girl there is.
          Perfectly respectable.

                    GENESIS
          With some pretty heavy
          baggage.

                    ROSE
          Are you kidding me? Guys
          love baggage. Besides,
          your baggage is, like,
          totally mysterious. I need
          some baggage.

                    GENESIS
(Picks up a fry, but doesn't eat it)
          Do you think he only likes
          girls who are . . .
          Christian?

                     ROSE
          I don't know. Probably.

                    GENESIS
          Yeah.

                     ROSE
          Seriously, do you like him
          or something?

                    GENESIS
          Me?

                     ROSE
          No, your imaginary friend
          next to you.

                    GENESIS
          We come from different
          worlds.

                     ROSE
          That's not an answer.

                    GENESIS
          I don't know.

                    ROSE
Oh my God! You do! You
like him! Hark, the herald
angels sing! You finally
don't like Will, the stoner
creepster loser!

                  GENESIS
Will's not a loser.

                    ROSE
Okay, just a stoner
creepster, then. Give me a
break.

                  GENESIS
He's not!

                    ROSE
He's not even hot. Oh, this
is excellent news! You're
finally over William
Fontaine!

                  GENESIS
Not "over." You have to be
"into" to be "over."

                    ROSE
You were.

GENESIS
No I wasn't. We're old
friends. It was just easy.

ROSE
That makes it grosser.

GENESIS
Why gross?

ROSE
Because he's like a
brother, then.

GENESIS
I wouldn't know. What do
you do with your brother,
Rose?

ROSE
Certainly not what you did
with Will down the shore!

GENESIS
We just kissed!

ROSE
(Holding hands to ears)
La-la-la-la-la. Didn't
happen if I can't hear you.

                    GENESIS
Why is it gross when I
kiss a boy and not you?

                    ROSE
I don't just kiss, my
friend.

                    GENESIS
Yeah, I know. Stop
bragging.

                    ROSE
You know it's true. Anyway,
you can do a lot better
than Will Fontaine. I'm
surprised he didn't make a
dishonest woman out of you.

                    GENESIS
He tried.

                    ROSE
Yeah, I know. Gross.

                    GENESIS
You should talk. Andy
Santos?

                    ROSE
La-la-la-la. Didn't happen!

(They both laugh.)

                    GENESIS
          Peter pulled me aside
          this morning to tell me
          he was glad I'm back at
          school.

                     ROSE
          I'm glad you're back at
          school. I had to fend for
          myself for two weeks
          amongst the dimwits and
          yo-yos.

                    GENESIS
          Of course you're glad.
          But why would Peter be
          glad? We're not even
          friends.

                     ROSE
          Maybe he feels bad for
          you.

                    GENESIS
          Gee, thanks.

                     ROSE
          Well?

                    GENESIS
          Ugh. I'm so sick of that.

ROSE
People are idiots. Just
ignore them. You know who
your real friends are.

GENESIS
I haven't been gone that
long. They're all looking
at me like I've sprouted
an extra eyeball or
appendage or something.

ROSE
Ignoramuses.

GENESIS
Yeah, well, it felt
different when Peter said
something. It seemed like
he really cared.

ROSE
Maybe he'll pray for you.

GENESIS
Oh, shut up, Rose.

ROSE
You'll probably have to
wait until marriage to
lose your virginity if you
go for that.

                    GENESIS
(Throws french fry)
          Shut up.

                      ROSE
          Shut up? Okay.

(She stuffs the rest of the fries into
her mouth, including the one GENESIS
threw at her.)

                    GENESIS
          Save some for the starving
          children.

(ROSE covers her mouth and mutters
something like "I'm shutting up.")

              GENESIS (CONTINUED)
          Okay, okay. Forget I
          brought it up. I don't
          know why he said anything
          to me. He's probably just a
          nice person.

(VANESSA enters stage left and walks
up to their table. She sits down next
to GENESIS and immediately starts
crying. The other girls sit,
awkwardly.)

ROSE
Uhhh, is something the
matter, Vanessa?

VANESSA
I just feel so sorry for
you, Gen. I can't imagine.

ROSE
Relax about it, okay?
Jesus Christ. Gen doesn't
need other people losing
their shit.

VANESSA
(Straightening up)
You guys got cheese fries?
(Neither answers.)
I am really sorry for your
loss, Genesis. I don't know
what else to say. I'm
sorry.

GENESIS
Thanks.

VANESSA
I tried to call you and
text you and stuff.

                    GENESIS
          I know. I saw. And I
          appreciate that.

                    VANESSA
          Will you please just tell
          me if you need anything?

                    ROSE
          She's going to be fine.

                    GENESIS
          Sure, Vanessa. Thanks.
(Beat)
          I think your friends are
          staring at you.

                    VANESSA
          Okay, well, I should
          probably get back to them.

                    ROSE
          You do that.

                    VANESSA
          I know we haven't been,
          like, close for a while,
          but you're still a really
          important friend.

                    GENESIS
I know, V. Don't worry
about me. Rose has got me.

                     ROSE
Damn straight.

                   VANESSA
(Gesturing toward her friends)
    They're waiting for me,
    and we're going to the
    game. Are you guys going?

                     ROSE
No chance in hell.

                   VANESSA
You don't have to be nasty
about it.

                     ROSE
Proud to be a nasty woman!

                   VANESSA
My mom wants to bring by
food for you and your mom
and sister if you need it.

                    GENESIS
Yeah, Ally isn't staying
with us right now.

                    VANESSA
          Oh yeah. Sorry. I did hear
          that.

                    ROSE
          Anything else?

                    GENESIS
          Thank you. That would be
          nice.

                    VANESSA
     (Lingering a beat longer than
     comfortable)
          Bye, guys.
     (Exit stage right.)

                    GENESIS
          You were kind of rude.

                    ROSE
          I'm sick of fake pity too.

                    GENESIS
          At least she knows my
          family.

                    ROSE
          Yeah, but no one really
          knows.

                    GENESIS
          That's right. And that's
          the way it needs to stay.

                     ROSE
          Oh, shit. It's five already?
          Where's my stupid brother?

(ROSE throws money down on the table
and GENESIS follows her offstage.)

(Lights fade.)

SCHEDULE

FOLLOW-UP

I sit up in bed, and my hair sticks to the back of my neck with sweat. Not my bed. Delilah's bed. Delilah's dorm. Dull golden light trickles through the paneled windows, and I look around to see three other empty twin beds. I think this building used to be a hotel or something because all the rooms have their own bathroom. Not so common for a dorm living situation. I'm happy not to be in a communal bathroom as I sit on her toilet and see blood has soaked through my underwear. I search through their cabinets for pads, but they only have tampons. Not supposed to use those just yet, so I wad up some toilet paper, stuffing it into my fresh underwear. I can't find a plastic bag or anything to put the old pair in, so I throw them away, tucking them under the top layer of trash so no one discovers the evidence.

Back in Delilah's room, I see a note taped to my bag:

Can't believe how much you slept, lady! Hope you're okay. Had to run to class. If you're still asleep when I get back, you're going to the hospital. ☺ Call or text pronto! Be back around 3.—D

Stayed the night? What? Is it really the next day? Did yesterday just disappear? Or maybe it didn't happen at all?

I'm still with Peter.

I wasn't pregnant.

Everything is normal.

If I wasn't leaking blood and so exhausted and so nauseous, then maybe I would believe that. But it must have happened. The whole thing happened. I must be here in New York City because Peter drove me to my appointment yesterday morning.

My phone blasts a thousand messages at me from Rose, wondering why I'm not at school.

I should have told her. I should not be doing this alone. I said I wouldn't tell, though. That's what I promised. My stomach growls and I remember I haven't eaten, well, in over twenty-four hours. How am I alive? I chug a glass of water and leave Delilah's room. It's 1:30 p.m. I can't wait until she gets back. I have to get home to Jersey. I have to figure out where Peter went. Why he left me at the clinic. Why I'm suddenly all alone again.

I pull up directions to Port Authority, and after a quick

hop uptown on the subway, I'm walking through Times Square, home to Broadway and the New Year's Eve ball drop and the M&M's store. Mmmm. M&M's. Can my first meal be M&M's? I don't think so. I bump my way through the sidewalks filled with tourists and their cameras and strollers and their general inability to walk in a straight line. I hold my stomach to avoid any extra trauma as I weave through the crowd under blinking marquees. My dad used to take me to the theater in Manhattan, though we never made it up here. He said all the good stuff was downtown. I took his word for it. I imagine myself onstage right now, in front of all those lights—red and yellow and blue. I'm not here fighting the crowd and the gray city snow. I'm onstage and the audience is tossing roses at me, and I'm smiling so hard I'm crying as I bow and blow kisses, and bow and blow kisses.

At the station, I purchase a ticket from the kiosk with my *emergency-only* credit card. I'll hear about this. I swear the grandparents must have the screen up on their computer at all times, waiting for me to purchase something so they can ask me about it. Hence paying in cash yesterday. That's a question I never want to have to answer. Not from them, anyway. The next bus leaves in twenty minutes, so I make my way to the waiting area. A boy around my age with a ponytail of dreadlocks and a dog in his backpack plays the accordion. His head falls forward and he picks it back up with effort. The dog whimpers a little. I sit in a hard plastic chair and dig out my phone to call Peter.

Again, I get the voice mail. Anger boils up from the new empty hole in my stomach.

"Fuck you, Peter," I say after the beep. Then pause for a

second because I'm unsure if I actually said that, if my voice actually came back to me.

I touch my throat. It has.

And so I go on. "Seriously? You want to know where I am? Port-fucking-Authority. Taking the bus home because you're a coward. Where are you? How could you do this to anyone? Let alone me. Let alone . . . me."

I choke on the word *me* a little and know I need to hang up. I really want to string together every nasty word and thought popping into my head and spit them at his face, but I'm tired. And I'm done.

The night before last, before he left my house, he placed the cash on the edge of my bed. Like he couldn't put it directly into my hands. Like I was microscopic. I didn't know if he'd come the next morning.

I board the bus and take a seat toward the back. It hasn't been easy to be with Peter since the incident. I don't even mean getting pregnant, though that certainly wasn't a stroll down the beach. But I mean the secret that got out. Things haven't been easy, but he stuck by.

Now where is he?

I'm suddenly terrified that I left too hastily. That maybe he lost his phone and maybe he stepped out and got mugged or something and maybe he's stranded somewhere too, trying to get home, and he thinks maybe I've left him. What have I done? What about the message I just left him? He's probably lying in a ditch or something and I'm going to be the one who has to tell Mrs. Sage.

But no. You know how you just know sometimes? I know he's not in a ditch. I know he left me at Planned Parenthood in New York City.

We arrive in Point Shelley in front of the Walmart. My head spins a little as I scan the parking lot, and I have to close my eyes for a second to regain my stability. I walk into Walmart and sit at a table in the McDonald's connected to the store. The fluorescent light buzzes in my eyes, and I know I'm too exhausted to walk home from here. I need a ride. I brace myself for the tornado that is my best friend, Rose, and I dial her number.

"What the hell, Gen! I thought you were dead!"

"Hello to you too."

"Seriously, where the hell are you?"

"I, uhhh . . ."

How to say it? Is my no-tell promise all null and void now?

"Are you okay, Gen?" Her tone softens a little.

"I'm sorta stuck at Walmart right now. In North Point. Can you come get me?"

"Walmart?"

"Yeah, Walmart."

"What the hell are you doing at Walmart?"

The word *Walmart* is turning surreal.

"I'll tell you later. I just, um, don't feel very well and need you to hurry, okay?"

She assures me she'll be there in no longer than a half an hour, and so I decide to finally fill my belly with the ever-so-healthy option before me. I didn't go for M&M's as my first meal, but salty, greasy french fries and a Coke will do just fine.

"Will that be all?"

The girl behind the register has a gap in her teeth and freckles so thick, they are more like splotches.

"Hi, Genesis," she says.

"Yeah." I realize I know her. "Oh, hi, Wendy."

"You look terrible!"

"Gee, thanks, Wendy."

"No, I mean, sick or something. You okay?"

"Yeah. I'm sick."

"You weren't at school today."

"No shit."

She doesn't respond.

"Can I just have my order?"

"Oh," she says, and looks down. "Sorry. Yeah. That'll be three dollars and nine cents."

I drop some change on the counter and wait for Wendy to fill up my cup.

"Not too much ice, please."

She puts the cup down gently in front of me next to a bag of fries.

"Here you go. Feel better."

I try to say thank you. Thank you to Wendy who works at McDonald's. She's always been sweet to me. But it just won't come.

"You missed Advanced Writing today. You're supposed to schedule your follow-up."

Follow-up? That sounds far too clinical for my liking right now. "Excuse me?"

Her eyes widen for a second like they're going to pop out, and I hold on to them with mine in an unannounced staring contest.

"Ms. Jones wants a follow-up conference for the papers we turned in last week. Like, one-on-one. We all failed as a class or something."

She blinks.

"Oh," I say. Still staring. I honestly can't think of what paper she is talking about.

"Yeah, she said none of us wrote from our hearts or our guts or something. We just wrote what we thought she'd want to hear. Then she was all squeaky and saying how none of us were brave. Sheesh. You know she writes romance novels? How gross is that? Can you imagine Ms. Jones, like, *doing* it?"

Someone clears his throat behind me.

"I've got to take care of the other customers now."

Fine, Wendy, I didn't want to stand here all day chatting about your theories on love. And certainly not the reason why I wasn't at school today. Or yesterday. I move out of the McDonald's and over to a bench by the main entrance, then sit, listening to the doors open and close. Open and close. I sip slowly through the straw, sometimes letting it get millimeters from my mouth, and then watching it plunge back down. I scratch lines into the wax on the side of the cup. I lick my lips. I watch security check receipts on the way out. I try not to think, really. As if that's even possible.

ACT I
SCENE 2

(This scene takes place in a crowded
high school hallway, between classes.
Students trickle through, slide books
from lockers, gather, gossip, goof off,
and so on, continuously around the main
action.

At rise, GENESIS searches for something
in her locker. She pulls everything out
and makes a pile on the ground. It is
clear she can't find what she is looking
for.

PETER enters stage right, passes her,
stops, does a double take, and then
watches for a second. He gestures for

her attention, but she is buried in the
contents of her locker.

He turns away, and this is the moment
she finds what she is looking for. She
stuffs everything back into her locker
and closes it, turning around to lean
against the wall in relief.

Now, she sees the back of PETER,
walking away. She starts to go after
him but stops, thinks better of it, and
walks off in the other direction.

PETER turns around one more time to see
her walking away. They don't ever see
each other turn back.)

                    PETER
(Reaching)
        Hey.

(Blackout.)

MONITOR

BLEEDING

Rose texts me as she pulls temporarily into a handicapped parking spot. I jump into the front seat of her hand-me-down silver Mercedes. The music blasts about three levels too loud as she backs out and exits the parking lot. She doesn't say anything, doesn't pry, but she fidgets. She likes to be the first to know what's going on, and clearly, I've let her down.

I keep my eyes on the passing auto body shops and liquor stores littering North Point, and I crunch on ice cubes. Wendy didn't listen to my request with the ice.

"You look like shit, Gen," Rose finally says.

"Thanks. Everyone seems to think so today."

"Well..."

The north part of town is a faded version of the city. A wasteland of boarded-up shops that never got it back together after the hurricane. Head south and it's much more conservative. There's more money down there. My house is right in the middle. Rose's, slightly south.

She parks in my driveway, turns off the music, and leaves the car running. In the new quiet, I stare at the house I share with my mom. Icicles hang from the rain gutter and drip into the soggy purple cushion on the wicker rocking chair.

"I didn't know how to tell you," I say when neither of us moves to exit.

"Tell me what?"

"What happened to me."

"What happened to you?"

"Well, I had an abortion yesterday." Rip-off-the-Band-Aid style. Cut to the chase. I think that's the first time I've even said the word. That eight-letter word. Peter and I were so good at dancing around it. A silent waltz.

Rose takes off her driving glasses and tucks them into the console between us. She puts her hand on my arm.

"What?"

I nod.

"You were pregnant?"

"That's how it usually works."

She drops her face into her hands for a second, then lifts back up into dead-on eye contact. "Does Peter know?"

My eyes fixate on the water marks dotting the side-view mirror. "Yes."

"And?"

"And he took me to my appointment yesterday morning, but . . ."

"But?"

"He left me there."

"What?"

I don't even believe the story myself as I say it out loud.

"I walked into the waiting room so he could take me home, and he was gone."

"Gone?"

"And he hasn't answered the phone or any of my texts."

"What the flying fuck?"

I unbuckle my seat belt, and feel sweat collecting in my armpits. I turn down the heat.

"Why in the world did you go all the way to Manhattan to do this?"

"He was worried about his mom."

Mrs. Gloria Sage: ringleader of our community's pro-life, anti-choice movement. The irony is not lost on anyone.

Rose shakes her head. She shakes it so hard I'm afraid she might hurt her neck.

"And why didn't you tell me? I would have taken you. And I would have taken you home."

"He asked me not to."

The head shaking continues like an uncontrollable twitch. "We couldn't figure out what the hell was going on with you. Our guesses were way off. What a piece of shit."

"No, Rose."

But wait. He is a piece of shit, isn't he? If you drive someone 58.2 miles away from home, put a blindfold on them, spin them around, and then tell them to find their way home, that's like the definition of a piece of shit.

"Yes, Genesis."

"Please don't get mad at me."

"I'm not. I just . . ."

"He didn't want anyone to know."

"You said that. But I'm your best friend."

"I know."

"Now what?" Rose asks.

"The nurse told me to rest."

"I'm not leaving you."

I want to ask her about school. About seeing Peter. But I hold off. Let the blow I just struck settle.

When we walk in the front door, my mom grabs me hard on my arms and shakes me. Ambushed. Her eyes are fire, and I am burning rubber, my body bending as she shakes until she finally pulls me in to her.

I guess she was watching me walk up the walkway.

I guess she was waiting for me.

I guess sometimes she pays attention to what is going on around her. I start to forget she's here, that she might still care about me. When a person stops communicating, you can only make up what they're feeling for so long before it becomes static. Right now, I remember I have a mother who might notice if I don't come home at night. There's nothing she can do, of course. Sometimes I really want to be grounded or punished or something normal.

"Genesis, I was worried about you. Where have you been? I was up all night."

The last time Mom reacted like this was when I fell off my bike on the way home from school right at the beginning of last school year. My bag got caught in the front tire and I flipped over the front of the bike and landed on my chin. My chest was covered in blood when I walked in the front door, and Mom jumped up and held me tight to her. Like she had some sense of my pain. That time physical, this time something else. She was wearing white and my blood got all over her clothes. I had to fight my way out of her embrace and call my aunt Kayla, Delilah's mom, to take me to the hospital for stitches. Mom hadn't started driving again yet. I got four of them. That night, Mom dished out two bowls of ice cream with a mountain of whipped cream and Hershey's chocolate syrup. My jaw was a little too sore to chew on anything solid for a few days and we ate ice cream for practically every meal. Her "cooking" instead of mine.

"I should have called. I'm sorry."

I say this, but there have been plenty of times I haven't come home and she hasn't reacted like this.

When my chin healed, and I got my stitches out, there was a little bit of a shift. Before, she was just kind of there. Enough there so I wouldn't be taken away from her, but far enough away that I had more responsibility than I probably should have had. But it wasn't long after that she got her job back in the file room at an insurance agency, and Aunt Kayla had to answer our distress calls less frequently.

"What happened?"

I suddenly very much want to hear her sing.

"Nothing," I say.

It's been so long and so quiet around here.

"I know that's not true."

I wait for the switch. Lights out, no one home. I've gotten used to the sudden darkening of my mother. I used to try to turn it back on. Flick flick flick her back into herself.

"You all right, Mom? Need anything?"

She's not switching off, though. Not retreating.

She answers. "You don't have to always take care of me."

"Well, if you want something to eat or . . ."

She shakes her head. "I had a Hot Pocket. There are more if you're hungry."

"I love Hot Pockets!" Rose says. "You have the best food here. My mom is all into quinoa and chia lately. I'm sorry, but chia pudding is not dessert."

"Chia? Like Chia Pets?" my mom asks.

"Um, yeah. Supposedly it's crazy healthy."

"Ally had one of those. A dinosaur."

"Mom, we need to go to my room."

She nods. I don't know what to do with her right now. She's usually asleep. We usually function on autopilot.

When we're in my room, Rose drops into my bed. "What was that? I thought she never cared when you don't come home."

"Yeah, usually she doesn't."

"Strange."

"Yeah."

I leave Rose and go to the bathroom so I can be alone for a second and look at my phone. Stare at it, really. Stare at it like a lunatic. Only a lunatic would keep staring and hoping for some kind of good news. Something new to hold on to. Because obviously I can't hold on to things that have already been said. There are no new words, no new signs, no new anything. Why hasn't he called? Isn't he wondering how I'm doing? It's not like I just had a tooth pulled.

Last Friday, after school, I waited for Peter. He was late to meet me, but I knew there'd been some extra planning going on for the Valentine's dance. I'd been so emotional lately, I was just ready to take care of our situation and move on. It killed me not to be able to tell Rose. I wondered if she could see any changes in my body. Or if they were only perceptible to me.

His condition: No one could know about this. Even one person beyond us and there was too much danger. He actually used the word *danger*. What am I supposed to do with that word? How is that supposed to make me feel when it's *my* body that changed? When I was physically carrying the *danger*? How could he want to keep something *dangerous* anyway?

I respected his wishes, though. Secrets really are like wildfire. But if you don't let them out, the secret wildfire burns you up.

I'll feel better Monday. I'll feel better Monday. I'll be fine on Monday. That's what I told myself to keep moving forward. To keep the fire contained and to keep the structure, my bones, standing.

While I waited, I saw him walking down the hall and laughing. How did he know how to laugh anymore? He was with Vanessa, and she was laughing too.

I've had to accept this. Their friendship. They have to work very closely in Student Government, and you have to pick your battles, right? But it was instant nausea whenever he'd say her name. *Vanessa thinks we should have a photo booth at the dance. Wouldn't that be cool?* Or: *I'll be a little late. Dropping Vanessa off at home before I come by.* You can imagine the physical reaction quadrupling when I would see them interact.

Peter never thought she meant to harm me. And it always bothered me that he didn't take my side. That he couldn't see how much easier things would have been for us if she had just kept her mouth shut.

I stood to block their path as they walked down the hall,

and I watched the laughter slide off his face. I wanted to dive for it. To pick it up off the floor and reattach it to him.

To us.

She said, *See you Monday,* without looking at me.

But Peter looked at me. And his look said *No, you won't see me Monday, because Genesis has other plans for us.*

Peter and I walked to his truck without talking. I was not trying to start *that* conversation when we had so much more to talk about. *That* conversation never went anywhere but around and around:

Him: *Why can't you let go?*

Me: *Why should I let go when she completely betrayed me?*

Him: *Sometimes there's more to the story.*

Me: *I know enough not to trust her.*

And so on.

But that wasn't the conversation of the day.

I looked at him. His face. His eyes. His mouth. Our mouths just fit. Sometimes I could have imagined kissing him forever.

How does that shut down so fast?

Fire spreads fast and ruthless.

Rose knocks on the bathroom door and comes in without waiting for me to answer.

"Jesus Christ," she says, and I see blood all over the inside my thighs.

"Rose, can I have some privacy, please?"

"Um, okay, but you were taking forever and I got worried about you."

"I'm fine."

"You don't look fine."

"I'm fine."

Rose presses her lips together, turns, and leaves. What does it mean to be fine? That's what we always say. Is it fine to run my course as a sloppy, bloody whirlpool?

I clean myself up.

I'm fine.

I'm fine.

I'm fine.

Say it three times, and make it come true.

ACT I
SCENE 3

(This scene takes place in a classroom.

At rise, TEACHER gathers papers.
Students enter and take their seats.

PETER chooses a seat in the front row.

GENESIS enters, and as she passes his
desk, he digs into his backpack so he
doesn't have to make eye contact. She
sits near the back.

WILL FONTAINE enters and sits by her.
PETER sneaks a couple of glances back
during their conversation.

VANESSA enters and sits near PETER.)

                    WILL
Hey, Gen. How's it going?

                  GENESIS
Going.

                    WILL
Tell me about it.

                  GENESIS
You probably know more
than most.

                    WILL
Everything okay?

                  GENESIS
Let me ask you something:
Have I come back to school
totally deformed? Do I
look like a different
person? Because the way
people look at me, it's as
if I'm covered in puke or
something.

                    WILL
Still the same old hottie,
Gen.

                  GENESIS
Come on now.

                    WILL
          What? You know it's true.

(Their interaction is playful.)

                    GENESIS
          I don't know anything
          about that.

                    WILL
          I'm sorry, but you know
          people are ASSHOLES in
          general, so just ignore
          them.

(Some people look in their direction
when WILL says "assholes.")

(Bell rings.)

                    TEACHER
          Vanessa, can you please
          hand these out?

(TEACHER writes "Magical Realism" on
the board.)

                    TEACHER (CONTINUED)
          Magical realism. Who can
          tell me what this means?
          Has anyone heard this term
          before?

                    BRANDON
          Yeah, when you brought it
          up yesterday.

(The class laughs. WILL high-fives him.)

                    TEACHER
          Then you'll have no problem
          reminding us what it
          means, Mr. Moore.

                    BRANDON
          Uh, we didn't get that far.

(More giggles)

                    TEACHER
          Okay, then, anyone want to
          help him out?
(Silence)
          What about Gabriel García
          Márquez? Who is that?

(PETER raises his hand.)

               TEACHER (CONTINUED)
          Yes, Peter, a man of
          culture and class, thank
          you for saving your
          colleagues here.

> PETER
>
> He's a Colombian writer. He
> wrote *One Hundred Years of
> Solitude*.

(GENESIS looks up from her doodling.)

> TEACHER
>
> That's right. Did you read
> it, Peter?

> PETER
>
> No, but I want to. I read
> *Chronicle of a Death
> Foretold*.

> TEACHER
>
> Ah, yes, I can see why you
> would like that one.

> PETER
>
> Really?

> TEACHER
>
> A very journalistic style.

> PETER
>
> I guess.

> TEACHER
>
> And was there magical
> realism?

>   BRANDON
> We still don't know what
> that means, Teach.

>   PETER
> I guess there's some
> surreal stuff happening
> in it, in a real kind of
> world. The brothel seemed
> kind of magical.

>   BRANDON
> I BET the brothel was
> magical.

(WILL high-fives him again; GENESIS
tries to stay focused on PETER and not
the clowns next to her.)

>   TEACHER
> Please.

>   PETER
> I didn't mean it like
> that.

(Some of the more jock-ish boys laugh
about his being a virgin.)

                    TEACHER
I know what you mean,
Peter. Okay, class,
let's go back to what
Peter said about surreal
details in a real world.
This is the key to
magical realism. And
we're going to start off
this unit by reading one
of Márquez's short stories
called "A Very Old Man
with Enormous Wings."

                    BRANDON
Sounds sexy.

                    TEACHER
Take the time to read it
to yourselves right now,
and try to find the surreal
and the real within the
story. The things that
seem magical and the
things that seem real.

(Class begins to read. WILL shifts
around, then raises his hand.)

                    WILL
        Can I go to the bathroom?

(TEACHER nods and points to the door.
He pops his hoodie up and leans toward
GENESIS.)

                WILL (CONTINUED)
            Don't take any shit from
            the army, Gen.

(GENESIS smiles and keeps reading.)

(After a beat, the bell rings.)

                    TEACHER
            If you didn't get all the
            way through the story,
            please finish for homework.
            We'll continue this
            conversation tomorrow.

(Class gathers things and bolts toward
the door. GENESIS walks by PETER again.
VANESSA lingers.)

                    PETER
        Hey, Genesis.

> GENESIS
>
> Oh, hey.

(Beat)

> PETER
>
> Did you like the story?

> GENESIS
>
> A lot.

> VANESSA
>
> I think it's disgusting.
> That angel creature or
> whatever he was is filthy
> and gross.

> PETER
>
> That's the point. That's
> the real and the magical.

> VANESSA
>
> Oh.

> GENESIS
>
> Yeah, it's pretty cool. You
> like the writer?

> PETER
>
> Yeah, I do.

                    GENESIS
          You like the brothel
          scenes.

(PETER laughs.)

               GENESIS (CONTINUED)
          Sorry.

                    PETER
          The man keeps things
          interesting, I guess.

                    GENESIS
          Sounds like it.

                    PETER
          Well . . .

                    GENESIS
          Well . . .

                    VANESSA
          Well . . . I think it's
          cool too. I just didn't
          like all the parts about
          the chicken dung in his
          feathers and stuff.

                    PETER
          Again, the point.

>   VANESSA
> Come on, Peter, we have to
> get to history.

>   PETER
> Go ahead, I'm going to be
> a minute.

>   VANESSA
> But . . .

>   PETER
> I don't care if I'm late.

>   VANESSA
> Okay. Well, bye, guys.

(She eyes both of them and leaves.
GENESIS starts to as well, but slowly,
and PETER stops her.)

>   PETER
> Are you . . . are you busy
> after school?

>   GENESIS
> Yeah.

>   PETER
> Oh. Okay. Never mind.

                    GENESIS
          I mean . . . Well, I mean
          I have to go see my mom at
          the hospital after school.

                    PETER
          Is she okay?
(Pause)
          That's probably none of my
          business.

                    GENESIS
          No, it's cool. She's fine.
          I'm the one who brought it
          up.

(Another pause)

                    PETER
          Okay.

                    GENESIS
          What I should say is: I
          guess I wish I wasn't.
          Busy.

                    PETER
          Yeah?

                    GENESIS
          Yeah.

> PETER
> Okay, I should get to
> class.

> GENESIS
> Yeah, me too.

> PETER
> I might ask you some other
> time if you're busy after
> school. Is that okay?

> GENESIS
> (Blurting)
> Do you want to come with
> me?

> PETER
> To the hospital?

> GENESIS
> Sorry, that's actually
> kind of weird, isn't it?

> PETER
> I don't know.

> GENESIS
> Never mind. It was a
> stupid idea.

> PETER
> What I should say is: Do
> you want me to come with
> you?

> GENESIS
> I think I kind of do.

(Beat)

(They take this in.)

> PETER
> Then, yes. I'd love to go
> to the hospital with you.

> GENESIS
> It's not a happy scene.

> PETER
> We'll make it a happy
> scene.
(GENESIS shifts awkwardly.)
> You don't need to explain
> anything you don't want to.

> GENESIS
> She's not doing very well.
(Beat)

But she didn't try to kill
herself.
(Another beat)
I'm sorry. Is this too
heavy? I know that's what
people think.

                PETER
I don't think anything.
I'll meet you by the
C-wing after school.

(Bell rings.)

                GENESIS
We're late.

                PETER
I don't care, do you?

                GENESIS
Nope.

                PETER
Good.

                GENESIS
If you change your mind I
completely understand.

                    PETER
        I won't change my mind.

(They nod at each other and touch fingers
as a way of saying good-bye. They're
both trying not to smile as they walk
away from each other.)

(Blackout.)

RECOVERY TIMES
MAY VARY

In my room, Rose is propped up against my bed on the floor, typing into her phone with her thumbs. I slide down next to her.

"Are you okay?" she asks, setting her phone facedown on the carpet.

Okay? Okay. Am I okay?

"Like, physically?" she says. "What do you need to do to take care of yourself?"

"Just rest, I guess."

Rose shifts. "Can I ask you something?"

"Yeah."

She pauses, looks at my stomach. "Did it hurt?"

"The procedure?"

"Yeah."

Did it hurt? I mean, everything hurts right now. Places that aren't even physical hurt right now. I think back. To the click. Slip. Pull. Snap of rubber gloves and metal wheels over tiled floor and my knees and thighs shaking.

"You don't have to talk about it."

"It was fast."

Rose nods.

"And it was definitely uncomfortable. Crampy. But not so bad, really. Everyone there was really nice."

"I should have been with you. Not him."

"I kind of just wanted to do it and then forget about it."

"Gen, you don't have to be so tough all the time. It's okay to talk about things."

My phone vibrates in my bag. Rose and I look at each other. Then I scramble to get to it before I miss the call.

This must be Peter. He must finally be trying to find me. We've all panicked before. We all know where we belong. I forgive him, I forgive him, I forgive him, I'm repeating in my head as I dig desperately for the phone.

But before my fingers can find their way to it, the vibrating stops. Rose takes the bag from me and slips the phone out as if it had been resting on top. She looks at the missed call, and then at me, and shakes her head.

Gran.

I knew I'd hear from her after the credit card use.

The phone rings again, in my hand, and I reject the call. I can't deal. I can't deal with anything. I can't deal with being alone. I can't deal with another person abandoning me. It's not fair. How many goddamned life lessons do I have to learn before I turn eighteen? I feel like I know some things. Why can't the universe or God or whoever it is who helps move things along cut me a little break here? Some people my age have never known anyone who died. Never fallen in love. Never broken into a million pieces.

"So, are you guys, like . . ." Rose doesn't finish her sentence.

"Are we what?"

"Are you broken up now?"

And then I lose it. Everything. Everything solid in my body turns into something gelatinous, like liquid just before it becomes Jell-O. The tears come from somewhere deeper than I've ever pulled them from.

"What happened?" my mom asks, appearing in the doorway now.

But I keep crying. Crying crying crying until there's no water left. And then I swear I'm crying air. Until there isn't any air. Whywhywhywhywhywhywhy?

I'm NOT fine.

I'm not fucking fine.

I'm.

Not.

FINE.

"I don't think I'm okay."

"You are," Rose says, and runs her hand through my hair. I'm not. I'm not. My mom is here. With us. With her arms around me and there are too many arms and hands and mouths and . . .

"No, really, I can't breathe, and it's like someone is crushing my chest. My heart. My heart."

"Can I make you some tea?"

"Don't go. Don't go. Don't leave me."

"I'm right here, Gen. Right here."

"We're not broken up."

Rose gathers my hair together and out of my face.

"We're not. People don't break up without a conversation, right? Can I still be with him, Rose? Is this just a fight or something?"

"What happened, honey?" my mom asks me.

"It's just a fight, isn't it? A misunderstanding?"

I'm on my feet now.

Rose still doesn't answer. She stands and faces me. My mom stays on the ground.

"I have to go to his house."

"I don't think that's a good idea."

"I need him."

"He abandoned you, Gen."

My mother tugs at my leg like a little girl. Tries to bring me back down.

My phone rings again.

"Why is my mother calling you?"

"What are you even doing in here, Mom? Why do you pick today to become involved?"

"Genesis, that is a horrible thing to say," Rose says.

Who cares if I still want to be with him after what he did to me? Our relationship is more than that. We're more than that. I can't keep this in. I can't. If I store all this now, then I'm sure I'll explode, so when all the tiny molecules of water that make up my body are stirring—no, whipping together—I let them. I turn into a tidal wave right there on my bedroom floor and all I can think to do is

knock
everything
down
in my path.
So I shove Rose backward.
As hard as I can.
And she stumbles to the floor.
"Jesus! Genesis!"
She collects herself and stands.
"Why the fuck did you do that?"
And I can't answer her. I don't know. I really don't recognize
anything right now. Nothing. Not the room I'm standing in.
Not the person in front of me. Not my mother on the floor. Not
the person in my skin. Everything spins together into gray
spiraling waves.
"What is wrong with you?"
I'm
Not
Fine.
Where is he?
"Hello?"
Is my mom really answering my phone?
"Mom!"
"I'm not sure. I don't know where she's been."
"Genesis, you need to calm down."
Then it's all arms reaching and people telling me which
way to go and buzzes and sirens and I have to find my own way.
I have to find my way back to him. I have to have the conver-
sations I don't want to. I have to go to him.
     And so I do. I run out of the house, leaving Rose and my
mom in the swirl.

ACT I
SCENE 4

(This scene takes place in a hospital
cafeteria. The lights are extra bright.
The few patrons sit alone, sipping
coffee, or picking at pieces of fruit.
PETER and GENESIS carry trays.)

                    PETER
          Table for two, m'lady?

                    GENESIS
          Why, yes, thank you.
          Something by a window,
          perhaps?

(They look around and laugh.)

PETER
Now see here, Madame.
We take the décor of our
restaurant very seriously,
and in order for you to
get the proper hospital
cafeteria experience,
we've built the restaurant
underground. So, I'm
afraid window seating is
not possible at this time.
But perhaps I can interest
you in a table with easy
access to the salad bar?

GENESIS
Whatever suits you.

(PETER slides a chair out for GENESIS.
She plays along with slight hesitation.)

GENESIS
Sorry you couldn't come in
with me.

PETER
Don't be sorry. There is
quite a magazine
collection in the waiting
area.

                    GENESIS
Sorry it took so long.

                    PETER
It's fine.

                    GENESIS
Sorry you had to come
here.

                    PETER
Stop. I didn't have to
come here. I didn't have
to do anything I didn't
want to do.

                    GENESIS
Why are you doing this?

                    PETER
What? Taking you out on a
date to this fine dining
establishment?

                    GENESIS
A date?

                    PETER
I admit it's not the most
conventional of first
dates, but yes, this is
our first date.

                    GENESIS
I've never been on a date
before.

                    PETER
Never?

                    GENESIS
I don't think so. I mean,
I've hung out in groups
and stuff, but I've never
gone to a movie or a
restaurant or anything
like that. With a guy.

                    PETER
Okay, then let's do this
properly.

                    GENESIS
Properly?

                    PETER
Yes, you know, because the
purpose of a first date is
to get to know the person
and see if you click.

                    GENESIS
How are you such a dating
expert?

                    PETER
I told you. There is quite
a magazine spread here for
a young guy like myself to
learn about the ins and
outs of dating.

                    GENESIS
I guess you had enough
time to become an expert.

                    PETER
I'm really not.

                    GENESIS
Oh.

                    PETER
Let's play Twenty
Questions.

                    GENESIS
Like—is it bigger than a
breadbox? That kind of
Twenty Questions?

                    PETER
Let's do the first-date
version.

                    GENESIS
You're making this up.

                    PETER
Of course I am. What's a
breadbox?

                    GENESIS
I have no idea.

                    PETER
All these years.

                    GENESIS
Okay, what's the first-date
version?

                    PETER
You ask me anything you
want to and I have to
answer. Then I get to ask
you something. And so on,
for twenty questions.

                    GENESIS
I don't know if this is
such a good idea.

                    PETER
Why not?

                    GENESIS
I don't know.

                    PETER
I guarantee client
confidentiality.

                    GENESIS
You a lawyer or something?

                    PETER
My dad is. But don't
worry. We're going to stay
on the surface in this
game. We have plenty of
time for the more
challenging content later.

                    GENESIS
What do you want to know
about me, anyway?

                    PETER
Wait, you're ready to
start?

                    GENESIS
I guess so.

                    PETER
Okay, then, let's start
easy. If you could eat

anything in the world
right now, not that wilted
iceberg salad you haven't
touched since we sat down,
what would it be?
(GENESIS thinks.)
Say the first thing that
comes to your mind.

GENESIS
Okay then, Indian food
from Curry Row in the
city.

PETER
Good one.

GENESIS
With my dad.

(PETER nods. They sit for a beat.)

GENESIS
There's a whole street of
Indian restaurants in
Manhattan. With Christmas
lights and hosts standing
out on the sidewalk, even
in the winter, trying to
herd you in. My dad used

to take us. He'd let my
sister and me pick the
restaurant. I'd pick based
on who had the most chili
pepper lights. Ally and I
would laugh when the
waiter offered wine. And
the food, well, I just
think it's the most
delicious food I've ever
had.

PETER
That's a way better answer
than I expected.

GENESIS
Low expectations?

PETER
That's the beauty of
Twenty Questions. Okay,
your turn to ask.

GENESIS
Am I allowed to ask the
same thing?

PETER
Sure, if you want to.

                    GENESIS
Okay, what would you rather
be eating right now? Or is
that chicken-finger platter
satisfying you?

                    PETER
You already asked your
question.

                    GENESIS
What?

                    PETER
You said, "Am I allowed to
ask the same thing?"
That's a question.

                    GENESIS
Not fair.

                    PETER
I'm teasing. My answer is
not as beautiful as yours.

                    GENESIS
So what?

                    PETER
I'd rather be eating pizza.

GENESIS
That's such a boy answer.

PETER
Guilty as charged.

GENESIS
I love pizza too.

PETER
Good, then you have the
job.

GENESIS
What job?

PETER
Job description being
worked out as we speak.

GENESIS
I don't want the job.

PETER
Oh.

GENESIS
No. Sorry. Not like that.
I kind of can't forget
where I am right now. Just
had a rush of reality.

                    PETER
          I know. I'm sorry.

                    GENESIS
          No, let's keep playing the
          game.

                    PETER
          You sure?
(She nods.)
          Okay, so we're on question
          three, then.

                    GENESIS
     Yes.

                    PETER
          Is this the best date
          you've ever been on?

                    GENESIS
(Smiling)
          Yes. Is this the best date
          you've ever been on?

                    PETER
          Second only to the time in
          sixth grade when I barfed
          on Lydia Pinkett while
          riding the Tilt-A-Whirl.

                    GENESIS
I remember Lydia Pinkett.

                    PETER
She broke up with me after
that.

                    GENESIS
That was fast. I was in
your class and I didn't
even know you were
together.

                    PETER
Fast and furious.

                    GENESIS
Ew.

                    PETER
Not meant to be. What's
your favorite book?

                    GENESIS
Slaughterhouse-Five.
What's your favorite color?

                    PETER
Blue.

                    GENESIS
A boy who likes pizza and
blue.

                    PETER
I'm a total stereotype.

                    GENESIS
I doubt that.

                    PETER
What do you want to be
when you grow up?

                    GENESIS
I have no clue.

                    PETER
Seriously?

                    GENESIS
Seriously.

                    PETER
Well, what do you like to
do?

                    GENESIS
It's my turn to ask a
question.

                    PETER
Fair enough. Go.

                    GENESIS
What do you want to be
when you grow up?

                    PETER
Are you going to keep
repeating my questions?

                    GENESIS
Maybe. If they're good
enough.

                    PETER
I'll have to take that
into consideration when I
ask my next question.

                    GENESIS
Should I be scared?

                    PETER
Oh, yes. Terrified. A
journalist. That's what I
want to be when I grow up.

                    GENESIS
For a newspaper?

PETER
What's a newspaper? Is that
like in the olden days when
people used to read their
news on printed paper?

GENESIS
I'm not sure this is going
to work out.

PETER
So soon? Well, at least
this lasted longer than
my date with Lydia
Pinkett.

GENESIS
We'll always have that.

PETER
Name three things you like
to do.

GENESIS
That's three questions.

PETER
No, it's only one.

GENESIS
Well . . .

PETER
I'm guessing you like to
read.

GENESIS
Why?

PETER
I've seen you reading at
school.

GENESIS
It's a good way to keep to
yourself.

PETER
I see. So, do you like it?
Or is it just an escape?

GENESIS
This is too many
questions.

PETER
I know. Back to the
original question. Three
things you like to do.

GENESIS
Okay, fine. I do like to
read. Not just to escape.

I also like to swim in the
ocean. And I like . . .
theater. Well, I used to.

PETER
This won't do at all.

GENESIS
What?

PETER
A girl who likes spicy
food, reading for pleasure,
the ocean, theater, and
lives life freely without
worrying about the future?

GENESIS
What do you mean?

PETER
You're *not* a stereotype.

GENESIS
Tell me about it.

PETER
I could if you wanted
me to.

GENESIS
Let's continue.

PETER
Whose turn is it?

GENESIS
Mine. Do you believe in
God?

PETER
(Considering the question)
Yes, I do.

GENESIS
Okay.

PETER
Is that a problem?

GENESIS
Is that your question?

PETER
Yes.

GENESIS
No.

PETER
Good.

GENESIS
So, do you believe in,
like, evolution?

          PETER
Of course! Do you think
all Christians don't
believe in evolution?

          GENESIS
No . . . I . . . sorry.
But, do you believe in
hell?

          PETER
Yes. Do you believe in
God?

          GENESIS
I don't think so.

          PETER
Agnostic?

          GENESIS
Yes. Is that a problem for
you?

          PETER
Is that your question?

          GENESIS
Yes.

          PETER
No.

PETER
Why haven't you told me
why your mom is in the
hospital?

GENESIS
I thought we were staying
surface.

PETER
You don't have to answer.

GENESIS
She had a bad reaction to
some medication.

PETER
What kind?

GENESIS
A new anti-anxiety. And
they thought she tried to
kill herself. I mean, I
did too, for a second.
Ally found her. But she
didn't. And it's not easy
to get someone out of the
psych ward.

PETER
Wow. Heavy.

                    GENESIS
I don't come easy, Peter.

                     PETER
I can tell.

                    GENESIS
This is a really intense
time.

                     PETER
I can tell that too.

                    GENESIS
What about you?

                     PETER
What about me?

                    GENESIS
Do you have this kind of,
I don't know . . .
baggage?

                     PETER
I can't say I do, exactly,
but I'm not perfect.

                    GENESIS
Is this what you want?

                    PETER
          Is that your question?

                    GENESIS
          Yes.

                    PETER
          (Grabbing her hands across the table)
          Yes. Very much so.

          (Lights fade. End scene.)

YOU MAY EXPERIENCE CRAMPING

I trudge through the snow toward South Point, where Peter lives. It's an easy walk in the summer, but now it feels like I'm forcing my way through a barrier I'm not supposed to penetrate. I'm burning. Tearing. Pushing. Forward. My blood bubbles with heat in the freezing-cold air around me. Finally, I stand outside the white picket fence surrounding his perfect little house and perfect little family, and stare at the shapes reflected in the window I know to be his room. I don't see his truck parked outside, but I walk up to the front door anyway.

His younger brother answers. He's taller than I am now, which happened sometime in the fall, and his dirty blond hair sticks up in the back like he's been lying down on it. He stands on the porch with me, holding the door open just slightly behind him. He looks from side to side, but not directly at me.

"Hi, Jimmy."

"Hey."

"Is your brother home?"

His eyes shoot down to his bare feet, which must be frozen out here. "No."

I try to peer behind him.

"I swear! You can look for yourself!"

He swings the door open wider, and I see the television on some kind of extreme sports show, and a scattering of snacks on the coffee table. Their huge gray cat sits on the back of the couch, licking her paws. She stops and stares at us with her paw suspended in the air. Waving, almost.

"Where is he?"

All Jimmy can do is shake his head and move the door back to its barely open position.

"Is your mom home?"

"No, I'm alone." He swings the door wide again. "Seriously!"

"Where is your mom?"

I feel like a private investigator or something, and I'm trying to break this poor kid down who obviously doesn't want to be involved.

"She's, you know, working."

Working. Busy Mrs. Sage with her community outreach and her church groups and her fund-raisers and luncheons. Work. Peter always told me my view on her was narrow. That really, she was doing a lot of good for the community, and that I was too hard on her. Me, hard on her? That's funny.

"What is it today?"

"Volunteering."

"Where?"

"Asbury Park." He breathes in deeply, and looks down hard into the floor. "I'm going to miss you, Gen."

"Miss me?"

I know what this means, and I don't know if I can bear to hear it from Jimmy Sage of all people. I steel myself, though.

"I'm sorry he's doing this."

I want to press him for answers. Press him for what he could have picked up from overheard conversations or maybe even what Peter has told him directly. But I just ask, "Can you please tell me where he is?"

"I don't know where he is, but . . ." He draws this last word out like he's falling off a cliff. *Buuuuuuuuuuuuuuuuuu* . . .

Maybe we're falling together.

"But what?"

I may appear calm to the innocent bystander, but I assure you, as I lose altitude from jumping off this cliff, the pressure builds and builds in my chest.

"I know he's with Vanessa."

And I splatter on the cold, hard dirt.

Jimmy swings his arms around me into a loose, awkward hug. I don't want to admit that it wasn't a good idea to come here. I had a body before I came to this door. Now I am a mess of broken bones.

I start to walk away and he grabs at my arm, so I turn back around.

"Genesis?"

"Yes?"

He takes another deep inhale and then says, "Is Ally ever coming home?"

"I don't think so, Jimmy."

He shakes off the answer like it's obvious he knew I would say that, and then stands a little straighter.

"I miss her."

I remember the two of them being the weird science kids who would collect bugs and study them. They were so excited when they found an American oil beetle. They both got blisters from some kind of chemical they emit when irritated.

"She's pretty happy in the city with my grandparents."

He nods. "I guess I'd be too."

"Lots of cockroaches to look at."

"You know cockroaches can live for weeks without their heads?" he says, smiling at me, all teeth.

"That's disgusting."

"Well, maybe next time my mom takes me to the Museum of Natural History, I can see her."

"Maybe."

I miss Ally. I miss how she thought powdered doughnuts smelled like ants, and how she never wanted to brush her teeth, and how she always wanted to watch old detective movies instead of cartoons.

"I'll let you know when she visits next, okay?"

He nods. "Do you want me to tell Peter you stopped by?"

I shrug because I really don't know. Peter feels like a ghost.

"Hey, Jimmy."

"Yeah?"

Taking a cue from Will Fontaine, I say, "Don't take any shit from the army, kid."

He smiles again, and I walk away.

Rose sits in her car at the edge of the driveway. She followed me here.

"You're going to get pneumonia if you walk. Please stop being so stubborn and let me drive you home."

Then I feel the wave again like I'm going to cry, but I fight it. I fight hard. I have to stop feeling sorry for myself. We sit in her car for a second. Catching our breath. My breath? Building my bones back up after the fall, when a car pulls into the driveway in front of us.

I duck for cover.

With my head between my knees, I say, "Who is it? Is it him? Does he see us?"

"It's not him."

Why would I hide from him, anyway? I came here to talk to him. I raise my head, but too soon. The car hasn't moved. It's perched at the bottom of the driveway like a hawk scanning for prey. Or: investigating which stalkers are parked in front of the house. It's definitely not Peter's truck.

"Drive! Drive!"

To which Rose peels out, away from the curb. A grinding, shrieking sound vibrates in my ears as I lock eyes with the person in the driver's seat: Mrs. Sage. She squints to see who sits behind the reflection in the glass, and when our eyes catch, hers widen with recognition as we fly away, leaving sparks, no doubt.

"Rose! Why did you do that?"

"I didn't think that actually happened! I thought that only happened in movies. You think I actually know how to peel out?"

I look back, and watch Mrs. Sage's car shrink and shrink until we turn the corner and head out onto the main boulevard.

And then I want to shrivel up inside my mortification.

"Where are we headed?" Rose asks me.

"Can we go to the ocean? I need it."

So we go. We drive back to my neighborhood and to the beach.

The wind picks up closer to the water. It flows over my ears like I'm running headfirst into someone's exhale. We slide under the railing, off the boardwalk, and over a snow-covered dune. I know there's a path and we're not supposed to walk on the dunes, but I can only go straight ahead right now.

Dead ahead.

Our sneakers crunch into the snow hiding the sand. We walk to where the water slides up to the snow, and then back into itself. I stare out over the gray blue until I don't know where the ocean ends and where sky, clouds, earth, space takes over.

Rose wraps an arm around my waist and nestles into my side. I wonder if I feel different to her. It did change. My body. When I was pregnant. Like right away my boobs pretty much doubled. But I'm deflating now. Back into what I was. The wind picks up again, and Rose's hair blows across her face. She withdraws from the sideways embrace and removes a long strand of hair out of the back of her throat. I close my eyes, and my own hair whips at my cheeks.

Does Mrs. Sage know what happened? Why we broke up?

We continue to stare forward. Out across the ocean, where everything blurs into gray.

"Remember when we used to write boys' names in the sand and watch the waves swallow them up and out to sea?" Rose says.

I don't answer her, but I do remember.

"What happened back there, Gen?"

"Nothing."

The ocean doesn't expect anything of me. That's what I love most about it.

"Nothing?"

"Do you think Mrs. Sage saw us?"

"Uhhh, I think we woke up the entire neighborhood."

"Oh God."

"It's not a big deal, Gen."

"Not a big deal? That we spazzed out so hard and ran away from the woman who already thinks I'm crazy?"

"You're right. That was terrible."

We take a second, and then both burst into laughter at the same time.

"That shit really does only happen in movies."

"Welcome to my life. Though I don't think it's a movie. I think it's an epically tragic stage play."

"Yeah, sounds more like it. What happened before the peel-out?"

"Jimmy said he was sorry Peter is doing this to me."

"Doing what?"

"Breaking up with me, I guess. He also said he's out with Vanessa right now."

Rose raises her eyebrows.

I sit down in the sand. It's cold and wet, but I don't care. Then something hits me. "Do you think he's getting together with Vanessa?"

"I honestly don't know. I could see it, though."

"Really?"

That is colder than the ground underneath me.

"I don't know, Gen. She's always had ulterior motives. You know that."

"I didn't put it together. Like, what if she told the story about my dad to break us up? To turn his mother against me and weaken us? So she could move in? Is that crazy?"

"Who knows? Maybe it is and maybe it isn't. That's pretty Machiavellian, though."

It makes sense. It makes perfect sense that she would let out my darkest secret to make him choose his family and their beliefs over me. And then she'd be there to catch him? Is this paranoid psychotic bullshit? Or is it something?

Rose picks up a shell and scoops up little piles of sand.

I know Vanessa liked him before we started going out. I know it hurt her when we got together. But so much time has passed at this point, right?

I stand and pull my hood tighter over my ears.

"Maybe not, though," Rose says. "Sometimes people aren't so calculated. Sometimes you don't know all the damage you're going to cause. People don't think."

Vanessa does. She thinks. And no one suspects it with her sweet-as-pie façade. She's just the kind of girl Mrs. Sage would approve of. From a good family. Promising future. Would that kind of plan actually work? Had she chipped away long enough that he'd just give in? Was I so much to handle that he needed to go someplace easier, safer, more conventional? Will she make him happier?

I let it go for now. Drive it out of my mind.

We walk back across the dune. Past the new condos by the shore to where the houses are a little bit more crumbly. Where people crumble and are just expected to carry on. Neither of us speaks. We don't get back in Rose's car. Rose doesn't fight me. The walk to my house isn't far from here. All I want to do is climb back into bed and forget about today. And yesterday. And the day before. Forget about the phone not ringing. Forget about Peter and Vanessa, wherever they are. Forget about old friends with cruel plans. Forget I have to go back to school tomorrow. I can't imagine what the hallways of the school look like. How any of my classrooms look. Anywhere I've seen or been with him has been erased.

When Peter came into my life, he patched up the places where everyone else left holes. Ally had just moved out. Mom was a zombie. And he was comfortable. Fun. Easy. Normal. Though I don't know what that means anymore. Because I don't think normal people do what he did yesterday when he left me.

Now that he's gone, I know nothing has healed under the patchwork job he did. There aren't any instructions anywhere on what to do when your dad dies like he did and then your boyfriend leaves you at Planned Parenthood while you're getting an abortion. Where are those instructions? How is it I still want to be with him? Who is going to tell me not to?

Not my mom. She's still pining for a ghost herself.

Rose, maybe.

Delilah, probably, when I clue her in.

I thought I wanted normal. I thought Peter and his family had normal. I thought it could solve everything. Now I just want to figure out my own version of normal. And rewrite the directions on which way to walk, which way to turn, when everything goes to shit.

ACT I
SCENE 5

(This scene takes place in a crowded
high school hallway, between classes.
Students trickle through, slide books
from lockers, gather, gossip, goof off,
and so on, continuously around the main
action.

At rise, PETER searches for something in
his locker. He pulls everything out and
makes a pile on the ground. It is clear
he can't find what he is looking for.

GENESIS enters stage right, passes him,
stops, does a double take, and then
watches for a second. She gestures for
his attention, but he is buried in the
contents of his locker.

She turns away, and this is the moment
he finds what he is looking for. He
stuffs everything back into his locker
and closes it, turning around to lean
against the wall in relief.

Now, he sees the back of Genesis,
walking away.)

                    PETER
          Hey! Genesis!

(She turns back. They smile at each
other and approach cautiously.)

                    PETER
          Hi.

                    GENESIS
          Hey.

                    PETER
          You in a rush?

                    GENESIS
          Um. No. Yes.

                    PETER
          Okay.
(Beat)
          How's your mom?

                    GENESIS
Fine. Not much different.
But maybe out today. My
grandparents are pushing
for it.

                    PETER
Good.

                    GENESIS
I hope so.

                    PETER
(Awkward pause)
Okay, I'm just going to
say it.

                    GENESIS
What?

                    PETER
I like you.

(Pause)

(GENESIS doesn't quite know how to
react.)

                PETER (CONTINUED)
I do. I don't care what
anyone thinks.

                    GENESIS
          People think about this
          already?

                    PETER
          No, not like that.

                    GENESIS
          Okay.

                    PETER
          You look skeptical.

(ROSE passes and interrupts.)

                    ROSE
          Gen! I was looking for
          you! Where were you
          hiding? Oh, hi, Peter.

                    PETER
          Hi, Rose.

(Yet another awkward pause)

                    ROSE
          Am I . . . interrupting
          something?

          GENESIS   PETER
No.   Yes, kind of.

GENESIS
Oh.

ROSE
Gen?

GENESIS
Go ahead. I'll be right
there.

(ROSE looks suspicious, but turns to
leave anyway.)

GENESIS (CONTINUED)
(Calling to Rose)
Save me a seat.
(Back to Peter)
So.

PETER
So.

GENESIS
I don't get this. It's so
out of the blue.

PETER
You really think it's out
of the blue?

GENESIS
Uhhhh . . . yeah. I'm not
your usual type.

PETER
What do you know about my
type?

(Pause)

GENESIS
Nothing. But I'd guess
less complicated.

PETER
Give yourself some credit.

GENESIS
Spoken like the prophet
counselor extraordinaire,
Ms. Karen.

PETER
She must read the same
fashion magazines I do
in waiting rooms. I
just . . . well, I . . .
I had a lot of fun
yesterday.

(GENESIS tries to hide that she is
very much enjoying what he's saying
to her.)

PETER (CONTINUED)
If we were in elementary

school, I'd ask you to be
my girlfriend.

                GENESIS
I don't . . .

                PETER
But I'm not going to.
Another thing the
magazines said was to
try to hang out again
to see if we like each
other. Not only was our
date fun, it was also
educational.

                GENESIS
I have to get my mom
settled back in today.

                PETER
Whenever you're ready.

                GENESIS
I can't do this.

                PETER
Can't now? Or can't ever?

                GENESIS
I don't know.

                    PETER
     Okay.

                    GENESIS
     This is a really bad time.

                    PETER
     I know. But I'm here. I'm
     waiting for you when
     you're ready.

(Lights fade to blackout.)

AVOID STRENUOUS
ACTIVITY

School today.

Somehow I kept myself from calling Peter last night.

Somehow he didn't call me either.

Somehow that was so much easier.

Why can't I glide through the halls today like normal? We could glide back to each other and never talk about these past few days, before everything atomized into little particles and started reshaping into pictures of things we don't know how to recognize.

I want to retrace back to when he was wrapped tightly around me, and everything felt safe. When the world shook up, and he held me still.

I slip into Advisory first period with my head tucked, and make a beeline for a seat in the back corner of the classroom. McDonald's Wendy is there, and she smiles at me. I think I smile back, but I can't tell exactly what my face is doing. I focus on *Slaughterhouse-Five*, my go-to book when I don't want to engage. Sometimes the firebombing of Dresden is easier to face than high school.

As I move through the morning classes, no one really says anything to me, but the looks are back. Those looks that feel like spotlights. You're blinded, while the onlooker sees you perfectly clear, illuminated. What do they see? What do they know? I keep my head down.

And then I run into Rose. Literally straight into her.

"Gen! Uh? In a hurry?"

It takes me a minute to focus and realize I can see everything clearly again.

"I haven't seen you all day, crazy lady. You avoiding me?"

"No."

She grabs my hand and ushers me into the cafeteria. It's pizza today. Rose usually brings her lunch, but pizza day at school is like a holiday feast for her. A break from the brown rice wraps and raw vegetables her mother usually makes her pack. Apparently others feel the same way, because the line is twice as long as usual.

Just missing one particular pizza lover.

"Is he in here?" I ask under my breath. It's only freshmen in line around us, so I'm not really worried about anyone overhearing, but just to be safe I have to ask. Rose gazes sort of spaced-out-like into the room.

"Who?"

"Don't be stupid."

She snaps back and faces me.

"Who are *you* looking for, Rose?" I ask.

"No one," she says, a little too quickly.

"Can you just tell me if you've spotted anyone I'd rather not see, please?"

"Coast is clear."

As I continue to scan, Will Fontaine enters the cafeteria. He lifts his head in my direction, then saunters toward us. He carries a skateboard with the word *Bones* on the bottom of it. I really don't want to deal with Rose and her bitchiness toward him right now. I wish some of his friends were here so he could glob on to them instead of me.

"Ladies?"

"Hi, Will," I say, deflecting.

"Hey," Rose chimes in too.

They nod at each other and smile.

"Yo, Gen, I'm so sorry," he says.

"For what?"

He opens his mouth and searches for words, stealing a quick glance in Rose's direction. "Well, I heard you and Peter broke up. I thought you two were going to get, like, married or some shit."

"We didn't break up."

Denial. Denial. Denial.

"Oh."

Someone from behind mutters to move up to the counter.

Will asks the lunch lady for three extra slices in addition to the allotted two per student. She gives him one, with a grunt.

"That's because she wants to eat the extra," he says, and Rose giggles. I look at her and then at the orange grease spotting up on our rectangular slices. Why is she being so friendly?

Will walks us to our usual table. To our collection of smart and rebelliously creative associates. The people who made Vanessa uncomfortable when Rose led me into this world. A world colored with blue hair dye and all-black attire. Preferring the Smiths to the pop stars. Will shoves the last of his slices into his mouth in one bite before bidding us adieu. He jumps on his skateboard for about three seconds before Mr. Padilla makes him get off.

"What was that?" I ask Rose.

"Oh, they're always trying to take his board away from him."

"No, not that."

"What?" She slides into a bench.

"The breakup? Is that what people are saying?"

Rose shrugs. But she has to know. I examine the faces of our lunch table companions. What do they know? They talk and laugh about stuff and send me sympathetic glances from time to time. Only Anjali, who I was in a play with in ninth grade, asks if I'm doing okay. Rose takes over the job of spokesperson.

"We're not talking about Peter or anything Peter-related today."

I don't know when we decided this, but I let it be for now.

They talk about the upcoming dance, and I know Peter is on the planning committee. We were supposed to go together. Everyone at the table agrees: dances are stupid.

Everyone except Stevie, who instead takes the stage for his courting-of-Rose routine we have to endure every single day.

"Rose, my sweet Rose, you want to go to the dance, don't you?"

"I just said dances were stupid."

The more she says stuff like this to Stevie, the more his uncontrollable passion for her grows. Or at least that's what he's said in past monologues.

"But, with the right fella, maybe you'd sing a different tune? Dance to a different beat?" He licks his fingers and slicks his eyebrows down before moving them up and down like a cartoon character. "Won't you let me treat you like the belle of the ball?"

She rolls her eyes and pops a piece of crust into her mouth.

"Don't deny it. It'll be a *gas*." Stevie makes farting noises with his armpit. Yes, people do this outside of eighties movies, I guess.

"Charming, Stevie," Anjali says.

"Whenever you're ready, my princess. Whenever you're ready. So, Genesis! What's up with Vanessa?" Stevie blurts out.

"What are you talking about?"

"Word on the street is she's getting too close for comfort with your darling ex."

There are many parts of this sentence that make me feel as if I'm made of porcelain, and someone, slowly and methodically, is banging a ball-peen hammer into my skin. Stevie, annoying armpit-fart-making Stevie, is already calling Peter my *ex*? And giving me information that is apparently common knowledge?

"What are you talking about?"

"It's nothing, Gen. You know how people like to start rumors." That was Rose. That was my best friend who just said that part. My best friend who should probably be clueing me in if there is gossip that, oh, I don't know, might confirm my deepest paranoia and also directly affect how I communicate with both Peter and Vanessa, considering my next class after lunch is with this pair of people getting *too close for comfort.*

If he's even here today. If he's not completely avoiding me. But, back to the slow and painful cracking of my armor.

"What the fuck, Rose? You've heard this too?"

Everyone at the table turns down like they're all mentally digging tunnels to their next-period class.

"I don't think it's true. I wanted to confirm things before I passed on the information."

"Rose? You don't think I might have wanted to know about this? You don't think it would make things slightly easier if I knew what people were whispering about?"

I feel some spotlights on me from other tables but I don't care. Until *this* occurs to me: "Do they know anything else, Rose?"

I know my voice is air-venom. Rose knows exactly what this means. That old eight-letter word. Starts with an *A.*

"Absolutely not," she whispers back.

I grab my book bag and bolt from the table.

Streaking through the hall, I hold the explosion inside with all my might. I'm not ready for this. How could I think I was ready to see anyone, much less walk into the potential disaster zone that is my next class? Advanced Writing with Ms. Jones, the secret romance writer, according to Wendy, who thinks we don't write from our hearts. I can't find my heart anywhere right now, so I think avoiding it altogether might be best.

I sidestep into the bathroom, and pray for solitude. A sick, twisted joke from the universe is what I get instead. It *is* empty, except for one head of bouncing curly hair, flossing her teeth in the mirror.

Vanessa.

She unwraps the ends of the floss from her fingers, and slides the string out from between her back molars. Then she spits into the sink and turns to me.

Here stands Vanessa, who used to be my best friend. Maybe one of convenience, but nonetheless a best friend. The one who let out the secret of my dad's death. The one who thought everyone should know it wasn't just any special heart attack, but a heroin overdose. Junkie's daughter. The one who thought I needed that added to my social résumé.

Hi, I'm Genesis, and you heard me right, my dad overdosed from shooting up more heroin than his body could handle, so he died.

Vanessa made sure you all knew that.

And she's used that to move in on my boyfriend.

We face off, gridlocked for a solid twenty seconds. I can't read her expression, though. It's not guilt. It's not pity. Both of which I would sort of expect from her. It's not smugness either. It's sort of neutral, really. Why can't she at least give me a real emotion to hold on to? What would she think about Peter's exit from the clinic? Does she know? God, it's worse if she does know. If she was in on it. If she encouraged it.

What if they're together now? Before I've even talked to him. When the last I've seen of him at this point was in the waiting room.

Before he left me.

"Hey, Genesis," she says finally.

I just stare. That tidal wave sensation from yesterday pools at my feet and rises through my body.

"You knew it was coming."

"Excuse me?"

"You had to know I'm much more his type."

So it is true.

The wave moves into my chest, and before I know it, I've crashed her onto the floor, and I'm tugging at her hair and scratching at her neck like a wild animal, and she's fighting me off, but not hitting back. I stop for a second, and we both pant for air. She's on her back, and I'm straddling her. My books are scattered around us.

"Get OFF me!" she shrieks.

I'm wet between my legs. Then there is a sharp stabbing in my stomach and I fold into myself and off of her.

"What the hell?" she asks. I see a shadow of worry on her face. "I didn't even touch you."

She's off the floor now, and I pull myself up too. I want to crawl to the toilet and puke my guts out, but I don't want to give up just yet.

We look at each other, and she still has a slight air of concern, but then she moves toward the mirror to examine the scratch marks on her neck.

"I can't believe you, Vanessa."

"What?" she says, so innocently I have a moment of doubt.

"What are you trying to do?" I ask.

"If you're talking about Peter, I want you to know he came to *me*. He said he hasn't been able to talk to you in months."

I let this trickle in through the cracks in my skin. And seal myself back together.

Vanessa continues. "You two are not meant to be, Genesis. Just face it."

"Face it? Do you have any idea what that means? Does he? It doesn't seem like he's facing anything."

"What are you talking about?"

"Oh, didn't he tell you?"

"Tell me what?"

I take a deep breath. If she doesn't know about the abortion it would truly scandalize her to the point that maybe she would be disgusted by Peter. I can't do that to Peter, though. Some loyalties die hard.

And telling Vanessa is like sending a mass e-mail to the whole school.

"Whatever, Genesis. You guys were never suited for each other. Everybody knew."

I hate her face so much right now. I push her. Just a little shove, bumping her backward. Then I gather up my strength and slap her across her face.

I slap her hard and cold.

She stumbles back into the sink just as Ms. Karen pokes her head into the bathroom.

"Genesis! Vanessa! What on earth is going on in here?"

Great.

I gather my things and head toward the door while Ms. Karen analyzes the damage I've inflicted on Vanessa.

"Uh-uh. You're not going anywhere, young lady. The three of us are going straight to Mr. Lombardy's office. He will figure out what we should do with you. Fighting? Really?"

"I didn't do anything," Vanessa says.

"Oh, really?" I say, with all the controlled fury I can handle. "You didn't do *anything*?"

"Nothing to get mauled, no!"

"Girls! Please! Save this for the office."

I shake my head and continue walking toward the door. Ms. Karen starts to protest again and I interrupt her. "Relax, I know. I'm going to Mr. L's office. I can't stand it in here any longer."

I can't stand it anywhere much longer. This bathroom. This school.

My own freakin' skin.

ACT I
SCENE 6

(This scene takes place in the
library. Tables are set with students
working individually on projects.
GENESIS, ROSE, and VANESSA sit at one
table together.)

                    ROSE
          Spill it.

                    GENESIS
          Spill what?

                    ROSE
          Don't play dumb with me. I
          saw with my own two eyes
          something between you and

a certain someone you
couldn't stop talking
about the other day.

                TEACHER
Ladies, this is quiet
time.

                ROSE
Sorry, Ms. Hamm.

(The girls watch until TEACHER is
preoccupied again.)

                VANESSA
What are you guys talking
about?

                GENESIS
Nothing. We're not talking
about anything. We're
working quietly during
independent study time.

                ROSE
Uh, no, there are more
important things to
discuss than the
Renaissance and
Reformation.

                    GENESIS
          Ms. Hamm thinks otherwise.

(Tries to signal to ROSE she doesn't
want to talk in front of VANESSA.)

                         ROSE
               Was he trying to ask you
               out?

                         GENESIS
               No.

                         ROSE
               Professing his undying
               love and devotion?

                         GENESIS
               No!

                         VANESSA
               Who?

          GENESIS   ROSE
     No one.   Peter Sage.

                         VANESSA
               What!?

                         GENESIS
               It's nothing.

VANESSA
You like Peter Sage?

GENESIS & TEACHER
Shhhhhhh!

(A beat)

(They feign working.)

ROSE
Not only does she like
him, but he likes her too!

VANESSA
(Raising voice a little too high)
Is that true?

GENESIS
I don't know.

TEACHER
Do I need to separate you
three?

VANESSA
Ms. Hamm, can I go to the
bathroom?

(She exits. Looking green.)

ROSE
What was all that about?

GENESIS
You're so dense sometimes.

ROSE
Uhhhhh . . . ?

GENESIS
She's only had a crush on
Peter Sage since
kindergarten.

ROSE
Still? Dude, I thought she
was over that after he
rejected her for, like,
three different middle
school dances.

GENESIS
I don't remember that.

ROSE
Oh yes. It was pathetic.
And then she went out with
Kyle Peacock.

GENESIS
For, like, a minute.

ROSE
I heard they went to third
base.

GENESIS
Gross. Anyway, apparently
she's not over Peter.
Should I go talk to her?

ROSE
You guys aren't even
really friends anymore. If
it's taken ten years and
something hasn't panned
out, chances are it never
will. Right?

GENESIS
Should I feel bad?

ROSE
Why? Is there something
happening?

GENESIS
I guess we had our first
date. Yesterday.

ROSE
What the holy hell? Why
didn't you tell me?

GENESIS
I'm telling you now!

ROSE
We've been through four
periods AND lunch and you
haven't thought I might be
interested in that little
piece of information? This
is huge. This is beyond
huge.

GENESIS
Calm down, Rose.

TEACHER
I'm not going to ask you
again, ladies.

ROSE
Wait a second. You told me
you were going to see your
mom yesterday.

GENESIS
We did.

ROSE
We did? We? You and Peter
went to the hospital
together?
(GENESIS smiles and nods.)
That was your first date?

                    GENESIS
          Yeah. We ate in the
          cafeteria.

                    ROSE
          You are a trip, Genesis
          Johnson. This is why I
          love you.

                    GENESIS
          It got weird, though.

                    ROSE
          Well, uh, yeah, your first
          date was in a hospital
          cafeteria. That's weird.

                    GENESIS
          That part was perfect. I
          think I was really weird
          today.

                    ROSE
          Like what?

                    GENESIS
          Like, I told him this is a
          bad time for me.

                    ROSE
Yeah, I guess it is. But so
what? This could actually
be the perfect time. Go
make things un-weird! Go!
Do it now!

                  GENESIS
Why are you so pro—Peter
Sage all of a sudden?

                    ROSE
Since I just saw how upset
it made Vanessa.

                  GENESIS
You're such a bitch.

                    ROSE
No, not really. I just
like seeing you smile.
Don't worry about Vanessa.
She'll get over it.

                  GENESIS
Who knows what will
happen? He's probably
going to realize what a
mess I am and jump ship
anyway.

ROSE
You don't have to know
what will happen. And
don't say that about
yourself.

GENESIS
I don't really get why he
likes me.

ROSE
Well, do you have
butterflies or whatever
other bullshit in your
stomach?

GENESIS
I totally do.

ROSE
Then go make it un-weird.

GENESIS
Okay.

ROSE
Now! Go!

GENESIS
Now?

                    ROSE
Yeah, why not?

                  GENESIS
Because that sounds weird,
not un-weird.

                    ROSE
He's next door. Go tell the
teacher Ms. Karen wants to
speak to him.

                  GENESIS
She won't buy that.

                    ROSE
Why not? No one will
suspect anything between
you and Peter Sage. Just
try it. Get him out of
class for a second and
tell him you like him.

                  GENESIS
This is crazy.

(ROSE scrawls out a note.)

                    ROSE
Flash this. They won't
know the difference.
Carmichael won't even look
at it.

                  GENESIS
I can't believe you're
talking me into this.

                    ROSE
Am I?

                  GENESIS
Why? I shouldn't do it?

                    ROSE
No, you absolutely should!

(GENESIS stands and makes her way to
the exit.)

                  TEACHER
Where are you going,
Genesis?

                  GENESIS
To the bathroom.

TEACHER
You have to wait until
Vanessa is back.

(VANESSA enters on cue. GENESIS points.)

TEACHER
Fine. Be quick about it,
please. The period is
almost over.

(GENESIS exits.)

VANESSA
Where's she going?

ROSE
To the bathroom. Takin'
care of business.

(She smiles as the lights fade.)

YOU MAY EXPERIENCE A
WIDE RANGE OF EMOTIONS

Mr. Lombardy is bald except for a few strands of hair draped across the top of his head. Busted blood vessels dot the skin on his face, and a thick gray mustache hides his upper lip. He reminds me of a rhinoceros: thick, with wide-set, beady eyes.

"I have no choice but to suspend both of you from school," he says without any trace of emotion. Again with the emotionless people. I wish I could channel some of that. I wish some of the emotions burning my guts like acid would just neutralize.

"But that's not fair!" Vanessa spits. "I was attacked!"

"Is that true, Ms. Johnson? Are you entirely to blame?"

I imagine Mr. Lombardy as a cartoon rhinoceros with a little monocle in addition to the mustache, asking me that same question with a British accent. *Are you ENTIRELY to blame?*

I don't answer.

Mr. Lombardy shifts his head back and forth between us, like he's writing his verdict via psychic wave.

A string dangles from Ms. Karen's skirt, and I want to yank it. Unravel everything.

"In that case," he says, "Ms. Stilton, you may go to the nurse and get those scratches on your neck cleaned up. Then return to class."

"I'm not suspended, right?" says Vanessa.

"No. You are excused. Ms. Johnson, you can go with Ms. Karen into her office, and we'll call your parents to pick you up from school."

Ms. Karen clears her throat and glances my way. I don't blame a rhinoceros for not remembering my dad is dead and my mom is not much better off. They have other things to worry about. Like avoiding poachers. And eating grass.

Vanessa stands, looks me straight in the eye, and says, "You've lost it. I've tried so long with you, Genesis. But you've lost it."

I fold my arms. Channel emotionlessness. Be one with the chair beneath me.

"You have no idea," she says. When I don't answer, she stomps out of the office.

"My mom is at work," I tell Mr. L. "I can take myself home."

He shakes his head and fills his cheeks with air, then waves his hand toward Ms. Karen to say that she should deal with this.

Suspended for three days. As if the kids at this school don't have enough to say about me already. Now I'm suspended and who knows how long it'll be until they find out about the other thing. If Peter tells Vanessa, I'm done for.

"Sit down, Genesis," she says when we make it to her office.

Ms. Karen has the kind of fluffy couch you get swallowed up by, with lots of colorful pillows. I've had to come here once a week since sophomore year. Anyone who has experienced death has to. Only one other kid at this school has lost a parent, though. Frederica Thompson. Her mom died of breast cancer. That sounds so much easier to deal with. All she got was sympathy. Not judgment for drug use or for how selfish that is with two kids and a wife to take care of and all. I told Frederica that once, and now she won't even look at me. I guess it was insensitive. One other kid lost a brother in a car accident. The drunk driver who hit him died too. If that driver had kids in this school, they might know how I feel. Except the only person my dad killed was himself.

"Ms. Karen, I really have to go to the bathroom."

I imagine myself bleeding all over those fancy pillows, but she doesn't let me go. And it takes me fifteen minutes to convince her I don't feel like talking today, and that as soon as I'm back from suspension I swear I'll tell her what's going on with me. I have to assure her it's all personal stuff and nothing to do with my living situation. Mom is fine. She works now. She takes care of herself now. I'm not the only one doing things anymore. I know she doesn't love her job, but I know it's good for her to get out of bed every day and go somewhere.

"And how is your sister?"

"She's fine, I think."

"Do you miss her?"

What kind of question is that? "Of course I miss her."

"Does it still seem like the right thing that she went to live with your grandparents and you didn't?"

How many times and how many different ways has Ms. Karen asked me this question? How many ways can I tell her my mom needed me? That there was no choice? I was determined not to lose her too. And that might have happened if she lost everyone.

I've tried:

1. She doesn't get along with my grandparents. The fighting would have killed her, and I don't need another dead parent. (*Sorry! I cope with sarcasm!*)

2. My dad was the only person my mom ever loved. She loves us, but theirs was that extra-something love. The kind that completes. That love left when he did. Part of her soul left. Part of her died. We had to keep some of the floor under her. (*Not grounded in reality*, said Ms. K.)

3. We have help. The grandparents give us financial support, and Aunt Kayla came over every single day, usually with Delilah, for a whole year. She didn't miss a day. Not holidays, not birthdays, not even something as mundane as a Tuesday. Never. She kept us keyed into the real world, in sync with the calendar that we had temporarily forgotten how to read. (No response, but I thought that was a positive sign.)

4. It wasn't too much of a strain on me. I kept up my grades, even when I had to miss a lot of class. Isn't that how you people measure everything? By how well we keep our grades up? (*That's an oversimplification*, she said.)

5. No one knows her like I do. That's especially true now that he's gone. I think I just knew she had to stay, and that Ally needed more guidance. And who better to provide more guidance than the two people who were champing at the bit to

mend the mistakes they made with my mom? Ally would become what they hoped my mother would. (She thought that one was very insightful. So did I.)

Anyway, now Ally gets to live in New York City and go to school where there's some excellent junior scientist program. Her interests have expanded beyond bugs. She's into chemicals and chemical compounds. And forensics.

"When is the last time you saw her?"

"It's been a little while. We're probably due up for a dinner."

"That would be wonderful. Do try to arrange that."

"Okay, Ms. Karen."

She had wanted students to call her by her first name. Thought it would help us open up to her and be on the same level. But the administration didn't let that one slide. She compromised by putting the *Ms.* in front. I don't mind Ms. Karen really. She means well. Being up in everyone's business is her job, I guess. I think it's getting to her, though. She always looks tired. And her clothes hang off her frame in wrinkles and clumps. It's kind of like we're sucking the life out of her.

I have to convince her I'm perfectly fine to walk home in this weather. That the long walk will actually do me some good. She lets me go, but puts her hand on my shoulder before I'm out the door.

"Genesis, something isn't sitting right here. I don't see you as a fighter. At least not physically. I want to know more about your motivations. I know you're suspended, but I want you in here first thing in the morning to talk. I'll send you home after that."

On my way out of Ms. Karen's office, I look down at her couch expecting to see a blood spot, but there's nothing there.

After a quick trip to the bathroom, when I'm finally outside I open my phone to call Peter. He's listed in my favorites, of course. Mom, Peter, Rose, Delilah, Aunt Kayla, Ally. Do I have to take him off now? How exactly am I supposed to proceed? How is a person supposed to move forward when they're still spinning from being left behind in the first place?

He's in class, but I want to leave a message. The air stings my bare hand.

"Look, Peter, I'm not trying to be a psycho or anything . . ." I mean, I guess I'm not. Though I do feel kind of totally psycho. "I'm just, honestly, super confused. I think after a year and a half, you owe me some kind of . . . I don't know . . . explanation or . . ."

I switch hands and ears and shove the frozen hand in my pocket.

"I got suspended today. I'm sure you'll hear all about it. Anyway. Call me. Please."

I can't say good-bye. I just can't. With my hands in my pockets and my hood up, I walk straight toward the ocean.

At the beach, the sun is at war with the clouds, glaring brightly through them, then retreating to the gray. I walk to the old dock and sit on one of the trunk-like poles poking out from the sand. The snow has been washed away by the tide. There are hundreds of shiny black mussel shells and a flock of seagulls swarming them. One seagull pecks at a Styrofoam cup before he squawks and cuts into the seafood buffet line.

I try to breathe in the scents around me, but it's like everything, even the air, is frozen and empty. In the summertime, it smells like sunscreen and hot dogs. Girls tie their hair in knots on their heads and untie the backs of their bikinis to avoid tan lines. I like to sink my toes into the wettest part of the sand. Peter used to look for new freckles on my skin after a trip to the beach and kiss each one.

You two are not meant to be, Genesis. Just face it. Vanessa's words. Is that true? Does all the good stuff get erased when problems come? Were we not fixable? Do we not get to try anymore?

I fight the urge to call Peter again. I want to be the one to tell him about what happened in the bathroom today, but that's not my job anymore. I'm now a girl who gets in fights and gets suspended. Peter never liked those girls.

What if I had kept the baby? Lots of girls do it and still finish high school and still go to college. I could have done it. Would we have gotten married? Would a baby have glued us back together? Mrs. Sage could have forgiven my *dark past*, and she could have babysat when I had to go to night school or whatever. Maybe the baby would have helped my mom get through whatever she needs to get through. Maybe it would have been just what she needed. Or this, the worst thought: What would my dad do if he knew what Peter did to me?

I can't do that to myself. Ms. Karen says it's not healthy to think like that.

If keeping the baby meant holding on to Peter too, why do I only feel relief? I can't come up with an image of holding a little baby that we made together, and watching it grow up and learn from us. It wasn't the right time for us. It should never have happened. And he agreed; I know he agreed. So why did he leave?

I am too cold to keep stationary so I head back toward town, but not before drawing a *P* in the sand with my boot and watching the ocean lick it away.

Should I feel sadness? The only sadness I feel right now is because I lost Peter somewhere in this. And he's already moved on? Is that what I'm supposed to do?

My phone vibrates in my pocket again. My heart stops and I stiffen.

Not Peter.

Delilah.

I should be used to it *not* being Peter by now.

"Hey, cuz," I say, catching my breath.

"What up, cuz." This, her usual greeting.

"Not much."

"You disappeared."

I guess that explains things. I've disappeared. I'm not here anymore.

"Genesis?"

"Yeah?"

"Are you distracted or something?"

"I'm just wandering around."

"I talked to Rose."

I know what this means. Rose, who seems to be able to keep her mouth shut about things like the fact that Vanessa and Peter might be getting together, but thinks it's her responsibility to inform my cousin of anything going on with me, has spilled the beans.

"Hello? Genesis, can you please talk to me right now?"

"I'm sorry. Did she tell you everything?"

"Yes."

There are things going on inside of me, they're kind of like earthquakes, or hailstorms. I can't break apart, though. I can't cry while I'm walking down the street.

"Are you okay?"

There it is again. That fucking question. How am I supposed to know?

"I got suspended today."

"What?"

I laugh. Like, deep-from-my-guts laughing. It cascades out of me, scaring a dog passing on his leash, which makes me laugh even harder. I can hear Delilah trying to get my attention, but I can't stop. Laughter and tears, and I can't remember why I'm laughing, which is also absolutely killing me.

And then I stop.

Take a deep breath. The air is an icicle jammed up my nose. Like a freak with a nail.

I'm silent.

"Gen? Are you there?"

"Yeah."

"What the hell happened?"

"I guess it all caught up to me or something."

I fight winter for more breath.

"What did you get suspended for?"

A few giggles escape like bubbles floating to the surface.

"What?" she asks.

"Well, I sort of attacked Vanessa in the girls' bathroom." She snorts.

"Yeah, you remember Vanessa? My old best friend? She's totally seeing Peter already."

"What!?"

I'm laughing again, but absolutely fucking nothing is funny.

"That's fucked up."

"What? That I did that?"

"No, that *she* did that."

"She's . . ." I don't know how to finish that sentence. What is she? I don't really know. In a way, once upon a time, I wronged her too. But that was totally different. Wasn't it? I messed that up. I wasn't straight with her about what was going on. I know it broke her apart, and I ignored that. "I don't remember much. I do know I was clawing for her throat."

"That's, um, weird? And kind of gross."

"Yeah, I guess."

"Oh, Genesis."

I shake my head.

"Are you okay? Does your mom know you're suspended?"

"I don't know. I haven't called her. I guess the school probably did."

"Yeah, maybe."

"Maybe."

"What do you need?"

"I don't really know."

"Well, I'm headed back to Jersey now. I want to see you."

"You are?"

"Yes. They asked me if I'd read at Café Solar, and I haven't seen my mom in a couple weeks, so I'm coming home for a long weekend."

"Tonight?"

"Yeah. Interested? It'll be mellow."

"I'm already downtown. I could kill some time instead of going home."

"Yeah?"

Delilah's been reading her poetry and stories at Café Solar since she was fourteen. She's sort of our small-town celebrity. Or at least everyone thinks she's going to be our claim to fame when she writes some bestselling novel or something. I love watching her read.

"I've got to stop home real quick, but I'll try to come early and hang out with you."

"Sounds good."

"And I have some good news to share with you," she starts, but I get a call-waiting signal. Heat rises inside my chest. Like burning. I look down to see it's still not Peter, but Rose.

"Rose is on the other line, Delly. Can I just see you in a little bit?"

"Uh . . . okay. See you in a bit."

I consider letting the call go to voice mail. I think I'm trying to be mad at her right now. I am mad at her. I think. Yeah, that wasn't cool not to tell me what was up. She can't be a selective big-mouth; she has to tell me when something like that could affect me.

I answer.

"What the hell, Genesis?" she says in her highest register. I have to move the phone away from my ear.

"Um, I could say the same?"

"Genesis, seriously, I'm sorry I didn't tell you what I heard. I thought it would blow over. Can we please move past that so you can tell me what the fuck happened in the bathroom? And where the fuck you are? I'm at your house with your homework. Ms. Karen tracked me down and asked me to bring it by your house, but she wouldn't tell me anything. All I've heard is what people are saying. That you are out of your mind."

Beware of Genesis. Don't fuck with Genesis. I catch my reflection in a window and want to pop my collar like a tough guy. "Did you see Peter when you went in for my homework?"

"You have to answer *my* questions first."

"No, I don't."

"What happened, Gen? I'm worried about you. Like, worried about your mental health."

"Rose, I'm fine. I'm downtown. Del is reading tonight at Solar."

"Ooooooohhhhh gawwwwd," she says, extending both words into about sixteen syllables. "What's the theme tonight? I can't take it if she talks about being burned to death again. That was too intense."

"I don't know. But probably something like that. Want to meet me there?"

"I guess so. I'm supposed to, uh, meet someone tonight."

"What? Like a date?"

"Something like that."

"Who's your next victim, Rose?"

"Oh, not important. You'll meet him tonight."

"Okay."

Mystery man. Great. Maybe that will take some of the focus off me for once.

"Hey, can I do anything for your mom while I'm here?"

"Is she home?"

"No."

"She's fine. She doesn't need anything."

I think.

I hope.

I can't really care right now.

ACT 1
SCENE 7

(This scene takes place in the school
hallway again, only this time it's
empty. GENESIS and PETER walk slowly.)

                    PETER
          We're not headed for Ms.
          Karen's, are we?

(Pause)

(GENESIS doesn't answer.)

                    PETER (CONTINUED)
          You're unpredictable,
          aren't you?

GENESIS
I'm ready.

PETER
What?

GENESIS
You said whenever I'm
ready.

PETER
I remember.

GENESIS
I'm ready.

PETER
Yeah?

GENESIS
Yeah.

PETER
Well, then I think I'm
supposed to kiss you.

GENESIS
I think that sounds right.

PETER
We may get caught and sent
to the principal's office.

                    GENESIS
You ever been before?

                    PETER
I haven't.

                    GENESIS
Me neither.

                    PETER
Worth the risk?

                    GENESIS
Yes. Yes. Absolutely yes.

(They kiss. Slowly at first, and
gradually more intensely.)

(Lights fade.)

TALK TO SOMEONE IF YOU EXPERIENCE FEELINGS OF DETACHMENT

After a couple hours, when I'm totally defrosted and on my third chai latte, Rose blows into the café and scans the room with giant eyes. She passes quickly over the bearded man playing sad songs on his guitar, through the sea of mugs, mismatched armchairs, and mason jars with candles. Then lands on me.

"Genesis. Good. I'm here first."

"First?"

I notice her cheeks are splotchy and there's a thin sweat mustache she hasn't wiped off yet. She doesn't answer my question or sit down; instead she says, "Are you still mad, Gen?"

Her voice cuts through the guitar player's soft melodies. I

motion to lower her voice a notch or two. Perhaps an octave while she's at it. "I don't like it, Rose. It was really embarrassing today."

"I know. I fucked up. I really am sorry, but please know I truly thought I was protecting you. Or maybe I was in denial."

A crossroads: stay mad at my greatest ally over a matter of principle, or move on and accept that she wanted to do the right thing.

But I already forgave her before she even said sorry. I need my full army right now. One soldier is already MIA (Peter, was he a soldier?), and the ranks can't break because of that. "It's okay, Rose. Just don't do that to me. I'm smarter than—and can handle a lot more than—"

"The average bear," she finishes my sentence, and we laugh.

This is what the first social worker said to me. After the medication incident with my mom, I had to see him at the hospital. Peter didn't know that's what took me so long on our "first date." This guy talked to me like I was a little kid. Told me I was smarter than the average bear. That always bugged me, but Rose helped me laugh about it.

The front door chimes, and Rose jerks her head toward the sound—focusing, searching. The sky has deepened to a dark blue, almost black. She has the same distance in her eyes as when we were in the cafeteria earlier today.

"What is going on with you, Rose?"

She pretends like she doesn't hear my question as she takes off her layers.

"Did you eat? I'm starving. I'm going to get some soup or something. Delilah here yet?"

"No. Just me and Mr. Sad Songs McGee. And no, I'm not hungry."

Her face shifts into something less scattered and more serious. "Are you depressed, Genesis?"

Ms. Karen asks me weekly if I'm depressed.

"Rose. Go get some food."

She smiles and pinches my elbow. Then hums a little too loudly as she moseys to the counter.

Delilah walks into the café next, and flops into a chair on the other side of the table.

"I want to hear everything. Seriously. Everything. But I haven't figured out what I'm reading yet, so can you just ignore me for, like, ten minutes? Please?"

I must be onstage in an absurdist play. All these characters enter and exit with quick lines and questions and I'm stuck in this booth. I think I've had too much caffeine. Rose is back at the table, and she splits a grilled cheese sandwich in half. "Here, share this with me."

I look at it, but don't think actors are supposed to share their food with the audience. I put a quarter of it back on her plate.

"Hey, *D* to the *L-I*-LAH," Rose sings, stretching a long strand of cheese from the sandwich with her mouth. "You ready to rock this joint?"

"Born ready, Rose. Doesn't it look like it?"

I can't help but feel further and further away. I don't know my lines. I don't know what I'm supposed to say. Delilah doesn't look up from her notebooks, and her black bangs stick to her forehead. The heat is up way too high in here.

Rose dunks the sandwich into a bowl of tomato soup and licks it off the bread before sinking her teeth into another luxuriously cheesy bite. "God! I love grilled cheese sandwiches. Why are they so delicious? Can you even answer that question?"

"Rose, can you shut up for a minute?" says Delilah. "I have to figure this out before Curtis says it's showtime."

Then as if on cue, the manager or manager-type with brown corduroy pants and a paisley sweater walks up behind Delilah. She looks down, then lifts her face up with a bright, glowing smile.

"Hey, Curtis!"

"You ready, darlin'?"

"She was born ready, Curtis," says Rose, enjoying herself a little too much.

"Yeah, totally," Delilah says, with a quick side-glare in Rose's direction. "Just putting my notes together. It's not seven, right?"

"Nope, a quarter till. We can push that time if you want. This guy never stops till I take out the big golden hook and drag him off."

"I'll be good with seven."

Curtis bounces away, and I see him take a deep inhale off the top of the coffee that a barista girl with rainbow-colored hair has poured for him. He makes ridiculous wafting motions with his hands, and looks like he is about to break into some glorious song or something, it smells so good to him.

"Seriously. Genesis. Spill it," Rose says. "What happened in the bathroom today? Vanessa looked like someone tried to murder her."

"Please," Delilah says, holding up her hand. "I want to hear this too. I just need a few more minutes."

Rose punches the air and taps at my face every few swings, breathing heavily and bobbing around. I nibble on the quarter of sandwich. Her face jerks toward the open door again, and in walks Will Fontaine, looking thoughtfully through the crowd. Great, I have to deal with this too.

Rose whispers quickly, "This is my date."

Holy blindside, Batman! Will Fontaine. Will Fontaine, who Rose gave me endless shit for, and talked for hours about how sexually repulsive he is, and how in the hell does he get so many girls, and why in the hell do I always want to kiss him, and how in the hell is it possible that WILL FONTAINE and ROSE MEYER are here for their public debut at my cousin's reading?

Now I'm catapulted up to the nosebleed section of the audience. I can kind of see the picture forming in front of me, way off in the distance. Excuse me while I focus my binoculars, because did he just kiss her on the cheek while she closed her eyes and smiled?

"I can see you're in shock."

"That covers the tip of the iceberg of what I'm feeling right now." I think I yell this down to them.

"Hey, Gen, this is cool, right?" This is Will. This is Will hollering up to me in row ZZZZZ, seat 1,000,009.

"Um. Yes?"

Rose's smile takes over her face.

So this is what was happening while I was obsessing over being pregnant and keeping secrets and having my stable ground fracture under me for the millionth time? Rose was running around with one of my oldest friends? Whom she ostensibly can't stand?

Delilah speaks now. "Shit, Will, I haven't seen you in forever."

They hug. And I'm spinning into the ground below me like a screw slipping into an already drilled hole. Quickly and easily.

Delilah looks at me with her eyebrows crinkling together behind her glasses.

"Genesis, we like each other. I'm sorry to spring it like this," says Rose.

I nod and want to laugh my head off. Just laugh it right off. Because actually, in the weirdest way, it makes sense. Perfect sense. Because nothing that makes sense is actually sensible, right? Peter and I weren't supposed to make sense, but we did. We fit. For a little while, anyway.

A group of Delilah's friends walks in next, and Curtis Manager-Man whispers into Sad Guitar Player's ear. I watch Delilah give her friends quick kisses on their cheeks, and they nod in my direction to say hello. Somehow their acknowledgment puts me back in this moment. Out of the absurdist play. I'm here to watch my cousin. My super-awesome amazing cousin, Delilah. She's wearing a plaid skirt with torn-up black tights and a faded Sex Pistols T-shirt that's not one of those stupid teenybopper department-store knockoffs. It's really from the seventies. She's very pale, with dyed black hair and black-rimmed retro glasses.

Looking at her, I realize how much I've missed her since she left for school. I never see Aunt Kayla anymore either.

"So, Gen, heard you really gave it to Vanessa today," Will says, grinning at me.

"I guess."

"She deserve it?"

"I think so."

"Good, don't take any shit from the army, kid."

Rose hands him the quarter of the sandwich I returned to her plate. He eats it in one bite.

Then I shift to Delilah. It's funny to see her back here. All she ever wanted to do was get out and get to the city. She sits on a stool with a scattering of notebooks and scraps of paper on another stool next to her. She jokes with the audience about how disorganized she is, then adjusts the microphone. The first poem is called "Murmurs." When she reads, it's like someone tightens a hand around my heart. Squeezing so hard I'm sure it will burst. Squeezing so hard the beats sputter out like they're fighting for survival. But the beats don't stop. Not even when they want to. Not even when they are so broken you think they can't continue. Her words pierce me. Words about longing and broken promises. Words about feeling absolutely trapped and then biting off your own hand to escape, but holding up the middle finger of your remaining hand to everything you left behind.

"I forgot how good she is," Will whispers.

Rose and Will are holding hands, and she rests her head on his shoulder.

Delilah reads, and I let my mind drift. I think about the worlds we land in and the worlds we move into. Delilah is building a new world. One she moved into by choice. Away from Point Shelley, New Jersey. And there was the world my parents tried to make for us here. But that one was more like a crash landing.

The story goes that my mom and dad met in the East Village in the nineties. My dad was writing plays and from time to time getting them produced. My mom was a Juilliard classical voice student by day, and by night, a frontwoman in a band, singing songs to broken hearts in the darkest bars. When they met, they became one explosion of art and music. My grandparents stopped supporting her, told her she was wasting her life away with my dad, and she dropped out of

Juilliard and into the scene full time. The drugs were a part of the picture, but Dad got in deeper than she did. Then she got pregnant, and panicked. She went to her parents for help, and they told her they would help if she left my dad. They compromised and moved to New Jersey instead. Closer to my dad's sister, Kayla.

Dad tried to get clean in New Jersey, but he would slip. He'd leave us for weeks at a time, back to get a taste of what he'd left behind. A heart can only take so much of that back-and-forth. He tried. Tried to build a new world for us here in New Jersey. But he didn't belong. They didn't belong. My dad left his dreams in the city and would chase back after them sometimes, but he didn't have roots anymore. He was a dandelion wisp of himself.

I realize that my mom faced the same choice I did. What if my mom hadn't kept her baby either? What would have become of them? Maybe it wasn't so easy back then to make the same choice I did—with my mom's parents being so religious, and it just being a different time. My eyes sting. And I push push push it all back, trying to shift into Delilah's words instead.

She's reading a story now. I catch pieces of it, but let her voice be cool air that fills up the room. I don't need to make sense of the words right now. I listen with my eyes closed. When she stops, there is applause.

The room winds around itself into words and sighs.

She's done.

I look at my phone.

There is a missed call.

From Peter.

AVOID ASPIRIN, ALCOHOL, MARIJUANA

I suddenly want to get very drunk. Like, puke-my-guts-up-in-a-gutter and make-someone-else-carry-me-home-for-once drunk. Hook-myself-up-to-a-tap-of-vodka-and-drown-myself-in-it drunk. I push my way through the people, through their heat, through their congratulations. Rose calls out "Wait!" but I just push. I push myself outside into the cold night that sucks my breath from me. One voice-mail message flashes at my fingertips like a bomb. What did he say to me? I decide not to listen. I decide to call him. I'm calling him and we're getting back together. And if not, I'm getting drunk. I either want to be drunk or be with Peter.

I'll try Peter first.

No time to think. No time to overanalyze if I should or should not call. I didn't have to think about calling him before, and I refuse to think about it now. I am a time traveler. It is one stinking week ago, when it was okay to call, okay to want him.

The phone rings, and my ear burns, hotter and hotter. I must be shooting steam into the part of the receiver I'm supposed to listen from. Peter Andrew Sage, you better answer the phone if you know what's good for you.

And then?

"Hey."

He answers.

The steam in my head disappears and my face deflates and I know that voice on the other end of the line, but it sounds so far away. Part of me must have believed he wouldn't answer. Whatever I say in this moment will go into his ear, but I don't have a clue what it is I want to say.

I forget everything.

"Genesis?"

That's me. Genesis. Okay, that's one thing I remember. And then I'm screaming. But it's one of those dream screams where nothing comes out. I forget how to make the vocal cords connect with my tongue and my lips, so instead I choke. Which pushes a gurgling sound out of my mouth.

"Gen."

Don't do that. Don't shorten my name and lower your voice to sound so sweet.

I still don't know what to say. I want to sink into him and hold him and smell him. But I don't think I'm allowed to sink anymore. Now I have to talk. Talk, not sink.

So talk, damn it.

"Aa-uhhhh." A sound crackles out of my mouth.

This conversation could almost be funny. Like two animals on a nature show, meeting on the tundra, grunting and snorting at each other until they know if they should fight or mate or pass on by.

I sort of want to do all three.

I grunt a hello.

"I can't actually talk right now," he says.

And then I know I want to fight. I want to rip into him. With claws.

"Peter, you owe me an explanation at the very least."

"Gen."

"How could you leave me there?"

"You know."

"But you showed up. Drove me. How the fuck could you just leave me there?"

Okay, this might not get me anywhere. Mrs. Sage doesn't like *language*.

"You need to calm down."

And then I am a volcano. Erupting fire and ash and rock. I'm not sure if I'm making words, but I know I'm screaming and screaming all the stuff I tried to say before—about what if I kept the baby. Would he still have left? And has he forgotten we made this decision together? And why did he do it and how irresponsible and how his mother can go to hell, until I realize the line is dead.

Dead.

I'm screaming at nothing.

What am I supposed to do? I meant what I said. How could any decent person abandon another human being, especially someone they care for? It doesn't take much to stay. It takes far more effort to leave. Leaving breaks inertia. Leaving means a whole new direction. A whole new energy source is needed to change course like that. You have to make a decision, then stand up, then leave. Peter did all of that. Made a decision, stood up, and left. In the dingy waiting room where Security makes non-patients sit. With its gray-lavender walls and daytime television and fluorescent lights. Trashy magazines and dead eyes. What did he read in the magazines this time? Nothing about first dates and how to win over your object of affection. He probably read how to make a clean break. Or six signs your relationship isn't working. Were there signs?

1. You don't see eye to eye anymore.

Did I see them too?

2. You want different things from the future.

If there were signs, why do I want him so bad it hurts?

3. You've become codependent.

I call back.

4. You've started fantasizing about other people.

And it rings and rings.

5. The quirks that used to be cute are now annoying.

I call back again.

6. You aren't happy.

I throw my phone down onto the icy sidewalk and kick my boot into a dirty bank of snow. Over and over I kick and curse until Rose and Delilah stand on either side of me and I capsize into them.

They don't say anything. They pull me toward Delilah's car. Then they both squeeze into the backseat with me. They don't ask me what that was about. I see Rose has picked up my phone and it rests on her knee. We sit there, and we can see our breath.

When Will taps on the window, Rose puts up one finger and sends him back into the café.

"He must be losing his shit in there," Rose says, and I laugh. Then they laugh too. They. These two most important girls in my life.

"Poor William," I say. "Surrounded by poets. Not a skateboard in sight."

Rose giggles.

"Can we go out?" Rose asks.

"Of the car?" answers Delilah.

"No, like, out-out. Like, to the city."

"Where in the city?"

"I don't know. Anywhere we can get totally shitface-hammered."

"It's a Wednesday night, Rose," I say.

"So? Don't people in New York go out every night?"

"That's true," Delilah says. "And I do have some friends throwing a party tonight in Brooklyn. I was going to stay at my mom's tonight. . . ."

Rose shoots lasers in Delilah's direction.

"Chill, Rose, I'm down to go if that's what Genesis wants."

I don't care what we do right now. All I know is, I don't want to go home. So going wherever we can get shitface-hammered, as Rose puts it, will be fine with me. It's not like I have to wake up in the morning. Suspension bonus. And it's not like I'm grounded or anything. Zombie mom bonus.

Oblivion beckons. I'm more and more like my father, it seems.

"Does that sound good to you, Genny?" Rose asks. I nod. Oblivion and anonymity. Maybe I'll even kiss someone. Prove to myself Peter isn't the only human being on the planet that I can like. That's what Rose would tell me to do.

"Ok, let's do it, then," Delilah says. "But I want to come back to Jersey tonight. So not all night."

"Deal!"

Delilah shakes her head, laughing, and goes in to retrieve Will and her friend, Wade. I open my voice mail and delete Peter's message without listening to it.

Then we're heading to a neighborhood in Brooklyn called Bushwick. Apparently it's really hip, with loft spaces and artists and stuff. Wade says it's the new Williamsburg, but that doesn't mean anything to any of us except Delilah, who nods like he's spoken gospel.

We roll into Bushwick at 11:45 p.m. Among industrial buildings and car lots, there is a store with a neon Open sign lighting up a window, though it's clearly closed. Above the door, the sign reads *Friends*. Two mannequin friends stare out at the lonely street in sunglasses and vintage dresses. Desperate for summer, maybe. Around the corner, there is a restaurant with a concrete façade and steamed industrial block windows. A man, hunched over and wearing a stained white apron, carries a garbage bag to the cans where two rats sit unfazed, chewing on trash. We park across the street. In front of the loft building where the party is.

We get buzzed in, then climb wide concrete steps that smell wet and moldy with a trace of beer. It's a girl named Kendra's twenty-second birthday. We step into the apartment and all the surfaces are covered with cans and lime wedges and empty bottles. The music is on far too loud for how few people are soaking it up.

Kendra kisses Delilah on the cheek, and thanks her about a hundred times for showing up. "I don't know where everyone went."

A guy with greased hair and a half-opened black button-up

shirt scoops Kendra away. "Actually, everyone is up on the roof right now. They're shooting off fireworks."

"Oh, shit!" Kendra slurs her words together like a Slushie. "We have to go up there!"

He looks at Delilah and raises his eyebrows. "A second ago she didn't want to go. This is what I'm dealing with now. But you guys should make a drink and go up to the roof. Someone drove to Pennsylvania and brought back a shitload of fireworks."

"Hell yeah!" Will says. Rose rolls her eyes and grabs on to his arm. Wade breaks into the vodka and mixes it with lemonade for all of us. I grab a second bottle and pour the contents down my throat. It burns, and so do Delilah's eyes.

"Easy there, cowgirl," she says, and pulls the bottle from my lips.

I open my mouth to protest, but then say to Wade, "Make mine strong, please."

Then we're climbing higher and higher, up onto the roof of the building.

The vodka moves through my veins. People huddle together for warmth while sparks of red and orange and yellow and green shoot into the sky and pop and sizzle and people scream and cheer and teeth chatter. Rose busies herself watching Will so he doesn't blow anyone's eyeballs out with fireworks. Delilah makes the rounds, saying hi to people I've never seen before. I can see the Empire State Building. My dad always said he loved that you could see the building from any part of the city. No matter where you were. You could always find your way home.

Tonight it's lit green.

I down the rest of my drink, mostly to keep myself warm.

Mostly. Partly to keep myself forgetting that phone call. Forgetting sounds best right now. Easiest, anyway. A shriek and a whirl of a firework go off in my ear. I move closer to the ledge.

A guy stands next to me, wrapped in a sleeping bag and smoking a cigarette. We catch eyes and he smiles. "Hey."

"Hey," I say, and think back to my idea of kissing someone else, but swallow that quickly. I look out across the blur of rooftops and lights.

"You know if you see them turn the lights out on the Empire State Building, you get to make a wish?"

I look at him again. He's looking straight ahead too. There's an orange light cast across his face and when he turns toward me, he becomes a half shadow.

"Is that what you're waiting for?" I ask.

"Taking a breather," he says, then stamps out his smoke.

We turn toward each other and for a second, we are locked. Eyes into eyes and a fluttering inside that could make me float away. I glance around for anyone to anchor me back down into asphalt and gravel. But I'm on my own. And where did that feeling come from, anyway?

"I'll leave you to it, then. Sorry," I say. Sorry for what, I'm not exactly sure. Invading his space? Interrupting his breather? Or maybe for feeling something that probably doesn't exist. Something I'm trying to conjure.

"I didn't mean it like that," he says, then turns his mouth into something angular and magnetic.

"I should probably find my friends."

"Okay," he says. I start to turn when he says, "But you should know that these wishes always come true."

"What?"

He gestures to the building and smiles again. Maybe I could get sucked into that smile and never find my way out. Maybe I'm imagining things.

"Your wish must be very important," I say.

"Why is that?"

"Because you're here."

"And so are you."

And so we are.

Just then the sleeping bag slips down off his shoulders. I reach out to grab it. So does he. But we both miss the fabric and catch hands instead. The smallest jolt shoots up my arm. I quickly retract as the sleeping bag drops to our feet.

I turn to look at the Empire State Building.

Still lit.

Pushing its light into a starless night.

I pick up the sleeping bag and hold it out toward him.

"You take it," he says. "It's freezing up here."

That electric jolt has transformed into chills. He's right. It's freezing. I spot Rose standing near Will, who is now lighting bottle rockets and runing in circles like a dog as they pop into the sky. She's yelling at him not to point them at the people on the roof.

"We could share it," I say without thinking. I want to take that back as soon as the words leave my mouth. I watch more shadows and splashes of light spray across his face, wanting to just burrow under the blanket myself until he disappears. Share?

"That sounds perfect," he says, covering us, flannel side down, slippery side up.

I don't say anything. I lean my body into his and let myself sink deep into the warmth around us and the booze in our blood and the breath and steam of strangers.

"Your drink is gone."

I look into my empty cup. "I think I drank it really fast."

"Do you want something else?"

I really, really do. I want something else. I want to know what something else feels like. I want to understand what it feels like to be without Peter. I want to show him I can exist without him if that's what he wants.

"Can we go together and stay under the sleeping bag?"

"That sounds fun," he says.

"But wait. What about your wish?" We both look again toward the green glowing building. I have a few things that I could wish for myself.

"I *have* been waiting for that." He smells smoky and lemony.

"Let's wait," I say, at the same time he says, "But it's okay."

We both linger on this.

"It's okay," he says again. "They turn out the lights every night. There's always tomorrow."

There's always tomorrow. There's always right now.

We make it back to the stairs to head down to Kendra's apartment. Delilah grabs on to my shoulder through the sleeping bag. "Where are you going, Gen?"

"Oh, hi, Del. This guy is bringing me back to the alcohol." My speech slips together.

"Who is this guy?"

I look at him. He has wavy brown hair that's kind of shaggy and greasy. His stubble is long, five days long, and his lips are wet like he just licked them. There's something dark and deep about his face before the smile takes over. I've never kissed a guy with facial hair before.

"I'm Seth."

"This is Seth."

Delilah's eyes look like flashlights shining into us, inspecting us. "I think I have met you before, actually."

"I think so too," he says.

"At school?"

"Maybe."

"We're fine, Delilah, we'll be right back up."

Then Kendra finally stumbles through the hatch on the roof.

"Delilah!" Kendra squeals. "When did you get here? Did you meet my boyfriend, Seth?"

"I'm not her boyfriend," Seth whispers to me. "She's just wasted."

He pulls me closer.

"My boyfriend, Sean. That's what I said!" Kendra belly flops into a make-out with the other guy, and order seems to have been restored.

I like Seth's arm around my waist.

Then Delilah says, "If you're not back in twenty minutes, I'm coming to look for you."

I give Delilah the sign for scout's honor.

"I'm serious, Gen."

I wave good-bye to her concern, and Seth and I continue our journey. He walks backward with his arms at my hips. I hop hop hop down each stair with his spotting.

We keep almost kissing, but then not.

I think that's what we're doing, anyway.

His breath hits my lips.

I hop away.

When we make it to the apartment, we find it empty. Everyone is still on the roof. I don't know how people keep warm up there. We mix more drinks with the sleeping bag draped over our shoulders like a cape. A cape for two.

"Your name is Jennifer?" he asks.

"Huh?"

"Delilah called you Jenn."

"Oh, it's Genesis. Gen."

"Genesis. Wow. Intense name."

"Yeah, my parents liked the band. My grandparents like the God stuff."

"Genesis," he says again.

I take a big sip of vodka-lemonade and it sparks and splatters through my veins. Our eyes hook together and he leans in toward my mouth. I block his path with my cup. He moves to my neck instead and I let him. My whole body tingles as I throw back the rest of my drink. Then we're kissing and diving over onto the kitchen floor, still wound up tight in our sleeping-bag cape. His breath tastes like cigarettes, and I'm turning into a puddle he's mopping up.

This is for you, Peter.

I lose myself in this kiss. There is an explosion and we are the only two people left on Earth. I push my body into his and run my finger along the button on his jeans. I need this right now. I am possessed. I need something else. Something new. He moves my hand away but keeps kissing me. I try again and he pushes me back a little harder.

"Slow down," he says, with his mouth full of my lips.

"I can't," I say.

"Can't what?"

He's out of breath.

"I just can't."

So am I. Breathless.

He scoots himself away from me and up against a cabinet.

"Oh." I fold my arms together over my knees. Reality creeps in.

"You want another drink?"

I nod. He fixes more drinks.

No alcohol. That's what the instructions said. And I'm drinking like it will restore everything that's left me torn apart.

No sex either. That's what they said.

Awkwardness hangs between us that I could mash up in my fingers like Silly Putty.

"Sorry, I'm kind of a freak right now," I say.

What I meant to say is I've completely lost control of myself. Peter held me together. Without Peter, I beat up girls in the bathroom and let men with facial hair kiss me on my neck and fix me drinks and then I push things too far.

"You're not a freak."

"I am. I'm sorry."

"Don't be sorry. I like it. I want it. Believe me. You seem really cool. And you're gorgeous."

We touch fingertips and lock eyes. Pressure builds in that stare. The air gets thinner. We get heavier. The pull gets stronger. The one you can't explain and can't identify as fear or excitement or whatever as it pulls you into someone else. There is no stopping it this time.

So I dive back in.

Into Seth.

And we swirl into each other like vodka and lemonade.

End of Act 1.

ACT II
SCENE 1

(This scene takes place in Peter's
kitchen. At rise, GENESIS drinks a tall
glass of something a little too fast.)

                    MRS. SAGE
          More lemonade?

(GENESIS and PETER exchange a look.)

                    GENESIS
          Yes, please. I guess I was
          really thirsty.

(MRS. SAGE purses her lips.)

> PETER
> It's fine. It's really hot
> outside.

> MRS. SAGE
> Come, let's sit down. I
> baked cookies.

(GENESIS wonders what planet she's
landed on.)

> MRS. SAGE
> So, tell me about your
> family, Genesis.

> PETER
> Mom.

> MRS. SAGE
> What? It's fine to ask.
> Isn't it fine to ask,
> Genesis?

> GENESIS
> They're not making
> fresh-baked cookies,
> that's for sure.

> MRS. SAGE
> Well, now, that's too bad.

                    GENESIS
Yes, it is.

                    PETER
Genesis, you do not have to
talk about your family if
you don't want to. Mother,
we talked about this.

(GENESIS shifts uncomfortably. PETER's
little brother, JIMMY, enters and grabs
three cookies off the plate.)

                    MRS. SAGE
We do not behave like
hooligans in this house.

                    JIMMY
No shit! I'm starving!

                    MRS. SAGE
Language!

                    PETER
Jimmy, this is my
girlfriend, Genesis.

                    JIMMY
We've met. I know your
sister.

                    GENESIS
Yes, of course. She came
to one of your birthday
parties, didn't she?

                    JIMMY
Yes! At the Museum of
Natural History.

                  MRS. SAGE
As I recall, no one came
to pick her up once we
were back home.

                    GENESIS
I picked her up.

                  MRS. SAGE
That's right. Late. I never
did meet your parents. You
said your dad was out of
town for business that
weekend.

                    GENESIS
He was a playwright. So he
had to go to New York
sometimes.

                  MRS. SAGE
A playwright. Hmm.

JIMMY
How come Ally hasn't been
at school?

PETER
You know the answer to
that.

JIMMY
I'm sorry.

(MRS. SAGE clears her throat.)

MRS. SAGE
Jimmy, I doubt your
homework is finished.

JIMMY
You're right about that!
That's why I came down for
brain food.

(He reaches for another stack of
cookies, and GENESIS laughs.)

JIMMY
Will you tell her I say hi
if you talk to her?

GENESIS
I will.

                    JIMMY
It's not the same without
her.

                    GENESIS
I know the feeling.

                    MRS. SAGE
Okay, Jimmy, that's enough.

                    JIMMY
Peace out!

(He leaves.)

                    MRS. SAGE
So, where did your sister
go?

                    PETER
Mom, can you please just
ask her questions about
herself and not about
everything I've already
discussed with you?

                    GENESIS
It's fine.

                    MRS. SAGE
Yes, Peter, it is fine. Does
your family go to church?

                    GENESIS
You didn't discuss that
part?

                    PETER
Genesis, why don't you
tell her about . . . the
book you're reading.

                    GENESIS
Um?

                    PETER
Or . . .

                    GENESIS
Something I . . . ?

                    PETER
Genesis volunteers reading
to elderly people.

                    MRS. SAGE
That's wonderful!

                    GENESIS
Well, I did once because I
had to for a class.

                    MRS. SAGE
I see.

> GENESIS
I don't do much.

> MRS. SAGE
I see.

> PETER
That's not true. You read.
You love the ocean. You
love spicy food. And
theater.

> GENESIS
Used to. But, anyway, what
good is that?

> PETER
You are thoughtful. And
observant.

> MRS. SAGE
I hope that translates
into a goal of some sort
in the future.

> PETER
You take good care of your
mother.

                    MRS. SAGE
Is she ill?

                    PETER
That's enough. Can this
interview please be over?

                    MRS. SAGE
I suppose.

                    GENESIS
We don't go to church,
Mrs. Sage. My grandparents
take us sometimes if we're
staying with them, but my
parents, or, uh . . . my
mom doesn't.

                    MRS. SAGE
You are always welcome to
join us on Sundays.

                    GENESIS
Thank you, Mrs. Sage.

                    PETER
Okay, Mom, we'll be
upstairs. Come on.

GENESIS   MRS. SAGE

Nice to meet you,   Door stays open.
    again.

(They exit. MRS. SAGE bows her head.)

(Blackout.)

DO NOT HESITATE TO CALL
WITH ANY QUESTIONS

I wake up sticky. Sticky from the inside out. My eyes are stuck together with makeup and crust. My mouth is stuck together with dried saliva. My skin is stuck to my sheets. *My* sheets. *My* bed. I'm in my bed, and I have no recollection of how I made it back here. I bolt up and look around for my phone, but I haven't plugged it in. All the contents of my head slide down into my stomach, twisting together until I feel like I'm going to puke.

Which I do.

Over and over.

Then I curl up on the cool tile of the bathroom floor. The pressure in my head swelling.

I remember the guy. The kisses. Just letting go. I remember sinking. Vodka and lemonade. More kisses. But I can't remember what I did. How far it went. When I try to think, my brain just pulsates inside my skull. Where is my phone?

I have so many questions and no phone.

And more blood in my underwear.

I call myself from the landline, but it doesn't ring, and when I click into voice mail, there aren't any messages. I dump my bag out. Gum wrappers, a compact with cracked powder chunks that stick to everything else in the bag. Lollipops from the girl at the clinic. A plastic water bottle with one sip at the bottom, which I gulp and feel sliding slowly into my body. Almost like it doesn't want to. A deck of cards. A piece of string. A scrap of paper with a number written on it, and a message:

In case you need rescuing.
—Seth

In case I need rescuing?

I need my fucking phone right now is what I need. *Language.*

I'm still in my clothes from last night, but it's not in my pockets or anywhere. Fuck. *Language.* Shut up. Shut up. Shut up.

What if Peter texts me?

Like that's what I should be worried about right now. I want to wash that other boy's kisses out of my mouth. I swish Listerine around my gums and tongue. I spit into the sink and watch the blue streak down the side of the bowl. My eyes travel to the pictures I taped up like a frame on the bathroom mirror. Peter and me on the beach with sand beards and sunglasses. Peter and me snuggled into the bed of his truck at the drive-in. Peter and me before the winter formal just two and a half months ago. I peel that one off and try to look for something in his face. That was the night of Rose's party. When we made the mistake in the bathroom. The broken condom that I just laughed at while Peter freaked out. Was there something I was missing before everything went down? His smile is perfect. Practiced. His arms are wrapped around me in a perfect side-hold pose. I'm not smiling. My eyes aren't on the camera.

Some pictures never taken:

Peter and me fighting about how much his mother didn't approve.

Peter and me when we ran out of things to talk about.

Peter and me at the abortion clinic.

I can't look at his face anymore. I rip any pictures with him down, and I tear the stack into quarters before throwing them into the toilet. The toilet that just held my vomit from a night I don't remember. And then I can't stand the thought of those two things mixing together so I extract all the ripped-up pictures from the toilet and spread them across the countertop to dry.

What is wrong with me?

I've been through so much worse than this. So much worse.

I try calling Rose from the landline, but get her voice mail. I look at the clock: 10:00 a.m. Fuck, again. I was supposed to meet Ms. Karen at eight thirty for whatever extra counseling she wanted to give me. I don't care, though.

I grab some ibuprofen from the pantry. That's where we keep it. Where Dad always wanted it. I remember sitting on this kitchen floor, the shake of the pill bottle, and Dad drinking half a carton of orange juice in one gulp to swallow the pills. Then cracking his elbows and shoulders and telling me not to get old. I swallow some orange juice as well, but can't get down as much as he did. It burns.

I take a long, hot shower and try to cry as the water hits my body. There aren't actually any tears coming out, though. I'm empty.

Wrapped up in a towel, I call Rose again, and again, I get her voice mail.

I start to dial Delilah but stop myself. I'm afraid of what she might say about last night. I need Rose on this one.

I really don't know what to do with myself right now.

And so I call my grandparents. A weird choice, I know. But I miss Ally, and I want to make good on my promise to Ms. Karen to arrange a dinner. A normal family dinner sounds like the perfect antidote to all this madness. I get their answering machine, which must mean I'm the only person left on this planet right now.

"Hello? Anybody home? Pick up if you're there. It's Genesis. I was wondering if you guys wanted to come over for dinner. Maybe tomorrow night? I don't know what we'll eat but maybe we can get takeout. It's been a little while. . . . Anyway, call me back . . . on the house phone."

And now who?

I think about calling my mom at work, but the reception is really bad in the file room. Also, I don't want to stress her out.

Maybe I should go to school and talk to Ms. Karen. She wouldn't care when I show up. She lives for talking to us. But instead, I decide I need rescuing.

And I have a special piece of paper promising just that.

"Hello?" His voice is muffled. Asleep.

He clears his throat.

"Hello?" he repeats.

I want to hang up. But I don't. "Hey."

"Who is this?"

"It's, um, Genesis. From last night?"

"Genesis! Shit, girl, you're not in trouble?"

"What do you mean?"

"Like, with your cousin?"

I rack my brain for what he could possibly be talking about, but since I don't remember how I got into my own bed, I come up blank.

"What?"

"I thought she was going to kill me when she barged in here."

"Barged in where?" Think. Think. Think.

"At my place. Are you serious? And your skater friend? I was sure that guy wanted to smash my face in."

"Your place?"

"My place."

"I didn't go to your place last night."

"What?"

"Weren't we at Kendra's?"

He's laughing. "Oh, shit. I knew you were drunk, but I didn't think you were that drunk."

I'm breaking.

"I was at your apartment?"

"Oh yeah."

I was at this boy's apartment? I've never been in a boy's apartment. I don't even know what a boy's apartment would be like. But I do know what happens when you go to a boy's apartment. My skater friend? Barging in?

"Did weeeeee. . . ." I can't finish this sentence. I don't want to know. I do want to know, but I don't want to say it.

"Oh, man, now I feel like a total creep."

Pieces:

1. I was at a boy's apartment.
2. Delilah barged in like a banshee.
3. Will tried to smash his face in.
4. Then somehow I got home.

There's a lot missing between #3 and #4. And a lot missing other places too. I just want to rewind. I want to fucking rewind. No one will ever rescue me now.

And now Peter will never want to get back together.

"Didn't we stop? In the kitchen?"

"Yeah, for, like, a second, and then we were all over each other again."

I do remember that. The pull. The not being able to stop.

"You left your phone here too."

"I did!" Maybe this is a rescue agency after all.

"Oh, man, Genesis, I can't believe you don't remember your cousin and all the drama. I'm sorry. I guess you found my note."

Shit. Drama with Delilah. I push my eyes tight together, and try to get an image. Even a fuzzy one. But I'm still coming up blank. I do remember her saying she would come looking for me if I wasn't back in twenty minutes. I don't remember much else, though. I was pouring back vodka like it would save me from myself. What did I do? Am I turning into my dad?

"Do you live near the party?"

"Same building."

"Can I come back?"

"Of course."

"For my phone." I don't want him to think I'm inviting myself back for anything else. Resist the pull. The pull probably doesn't even exist in the daylight.

"Okay then, you know where I live. Actually you probably don't."

His voice is low and smooth.

"Yeah. No."

"I'll be around, but I have class at four."

That will be perfect. There and back. No lingering. "I can get there before then."

He gives me his address and directions, and now I have to find my way to Brooklyn on the train to get my stupid phone and see some boy I don't remember having sex with because this is my life now. I sleep with random boys and then my cousin goes psycho and my friends try to beat him up even though it was probably my fault. Really leading the model existence right now.

And what was the reason not to have sex after an abortion? I don't know if they gave me one. Is that why I'm bleeding again? What if I can never have children now? Peter won't want me if I can't have children. I really really really hope I haven't fucked up my life even more than it already is.

The phone rings, and I let the machine pick it up.

"Genesis? Genesis? Are you there?" It's my grandmother. "Genesis, you just rang me. Where are you? Okay, well, I think tomorrow sounds great. Gen? Pick up if you're home. Okay, well, we'll see you tomorrow, honey. I'll try your cell. Bye now."

Instructions for the afternoon:

1. Get to Brooklyn.

2. Get phone back from strange boy.

3. Find way back home.

4. Call Rose and get all the facts straight.
5. Put everything back into a normal order.
I can do this. These are instructions I can handle.

Bushwick looks different in the sunlight. It looks naked. Like what you don't want to see after a night of drinking. No leaves on what few trees have sprouted through the cement. Graffiti-covered industrial buildings. Car alarms screaming to turn out the lights and go back to sleep even at two thirty in the afternoon. I draw my hood tighter as the foggy image of last night starts to clear. The trash has been picked up in front of the restaurant across the street. I scan for #431 on the cold metal box.

The door buzzes, and I push it open. I remember these concrete stairs, this faint scent of mold and beer. I see red plastic cups in corners as I climb up to the fourth floor. The hallways are wide and rough with exposed drywall and unfinished wood floors. I see an open door down the hallway, and a head of wet, shaggy hair pokes out.

Seth.

He's actually pretty cute. I guess I wasn't totally blind drunk last night.

"Hey," he says, stepping into the hallway. He's wearing a plaid robe that exposes a smooth, bare chest. He leans in toward me. To kiss? I draw back.

"Okay, I get it. One-time thing," he says, laughing.

I can't figure out what's so funny about a one-time thing. I don't run around and do one-time things. But I can play along.

"Yeah. One-time thing. Do you have my phone?"

"Come on in."

I don't really want to *come on in*. I just want my phone and I want to get the hell back to New Jersey and then collapse with Rose and hear about my night last night. That's the plan. That's all I want from today.

Stay the course.

"No offense, but you look a little worse for wear," he says. "Do you want some coffee?"

I can smell it brewing. It might help with my headache. He puts his hands up in the air. "I promise I won't try anything! I have to leave in about a half hour."

He guides me to his couch and puts a blanket over my knees, making a big pretend fuss to fit it perfectly. I try not to laugh at his grand gestures. He could be a medieval warrior in stature, reincarnated as a scruffy, laid-back Brooklyn dude. It's a confusing combination—like there's a lot of strength in his presence, but it's not intimidating. It's fun. I have to stop looking at him. So I look around his apartment: hanging behind me are three guitars, and the room is covered in Christmas lights. He has an orange construction cone with a lightbulb sticking out of the top, and the wall has two huge canvases splattered with bright colored paint. The wood floor is a little dusty, but the apartment is comfortable. I lean back into the arm of the couch and gather the blanket up tighter.

"Are you hungry?" he asks from the kitchen.

"I'm okay."

Not sure anything would stay down anyway.

He bounces around the kitchen, putting dishes away. I see him toss out an empty bottle of vodka and can taste it in the back of my throat all the way down to my stomach. There's an exposed brick wall across from me covered in tiny black frames with vintage portraits. The apartment is warm despite the icy-looking industrial window taking over most of one side of the room.

"Sorry, my roommate has been on my case lately about dishes. I'll be one sec."

Seth moves around with ease. Like the feeling of last night in his skin is something he enjoys. I, on the other hand, want to puke it all out and get back to what I know to be safe. But seriously, what is that?

Detached infatuation. Another one of Ms. Karen's jargon labels for me.

I send a silent apology to Ms. Karen for ditching her today. I bet she's called. I need that phone back. I should text my grandma to confirm tomorrow. She's probably called fifty more times since the last message. She's like Rose in that way.

"I never answered your question," he says, pouring the coffee. "Milk and sugar?"

"Black. What question?"

"Did we . . . ?" He drags out the *we-eeeeee* like I did on the phone earlier.

"What?"

"You asked me if we, y'know . . . had sex."

"Yeah, didn't we?"

"Wow, I mean, I know I'm not like Romeo or anything, but I would hope even a blackout drunk chick would remember something if it'd happened."

"It did or it didn't?" And by the way, he *is* kind of like Romeo. Handsome. And, like, impulsive. And I have to stop.

He smiles. I want to kiss him. No I don't.

"Nope."

"Why not?"

"Oh, now you want it?"

"No!"

His hands go up again, then he leans back into the cushions and puts his legs up on top of my knees.

"You were too drunk, Genesis. I think you're hot and all, but I'm not going to take advantage of you."

"I just got out of a relationship." Let that cat out of the bag.

"You told me."

"I did?"

He nods.

"What else did I tell you?"

"That you can't have sex for three weeks."

Now I laugh. "I said that?"

"Over and over."

I put my head down into my hands and can smell the lemon soap on his legs.

"Can I see you in three weeks?" he says, winking.

I shake my head. Then I hear a bus screech up outside, let out a gust of air like a sigh, and start beeping. Why in the world would he ever want to see me again? It seems like all I did was royally embarrass myself.

"I'm an idiot."

He straightens up and takes his legs off mine. "Don't be silly."

"No, really, I'm a big fat idiot."

"Hey, now. Everyone gets drunk and stupid sometimes."

"I don't. I mean, not usually."

"Welcome to Bushwick. Land of drunk and stupid."

I shake my head again, and bend my knees into my chest.

"You weren't that bad, Gen. I had a lot of fun with you."

"You did?"

"Come on. It seemed like you were having fun. Don't tell me I imagined the whole thing."

Did I imagine the whole thing? No, I un-imagined the whole thing by drinking everything in my path to black out. "How old are you, Seth?"

"Well, I tell people I'm twenty-one."

"But?"

"But I'm really nineteen. The facial hair helps."

More relief escapes my body like the air from the bus. That's not so bad.

"I'm seventeen."

He acts like he's about to spit his coffee out, but he swallows and smiles instead. I can't tell if the gesture is a joke or not. "Well, good thing I didn't take advantage of you, then!"

"Do you think I'm an idiot?"

"No. You behave much better than I do. Anyway, when do you turn eighteen?"

"Oh God. Sunday. I almost forgot."

"No one forgets their birthday. That's such a cliché."

"I did until now."

"Sunday is in three days."

"Oh God."

He looks at the clock. "Shit. I have to get to class."

His face shifts a little, and I can't quite tell what I'm detecting.

"Okay, so can I have my phone?"

"Oh, right, the phone. That's why you came here."

He leaves and I flutter for a second. A split second. An untrustworthy second. That's why I came here. To get the phone. Not to get swept back into the imaginary. This guy is really nice and I probably won't ever see him again, and I shouldn't anyway because he has an apartment and I live with my mom, but I don't know. Do I want to see him again? He holds the phone out and when I grab it, he doesn't let go. We playfully tug it back and forth for a second.

"Can we please hang out again when you're eighteen?"

Too soon, too soon, too soon. But I'm trying to figure out how to take his compliments.

"I don't know." (Meaning: I don't know ANYTHING.)

He shakes his head, and I pull the blanket up to my shoulders.

"Will you wait for me to get dressed? I'll walk you to the train."

I nod.

"I'll put some music on for you while I get ready."

He puts on Johnny Cash (because, DUH), and I finish my coffee. I think about my aunt Kayla telling her story of meeting Johnny Cash in a hotel elevator in Manhattan. And how she bumped into him later and he said, "Hi, Kayla," like they were old friends, and how she said she could have died right then and there.

I don't tell Seth that story. Instead, he chatters on and on to me about his acting program and how he wants to be in something that's not a part of his school so he's auditioning for some non-union off-Broadway thing tomorrow that's probably not any good, but he is just so irritated by the students at NYU right now that he needs to see what other types of people are making theater in the city.

"How did you find this audition?"

He walks back into the room. He still doesn't have a shirt on, but now he has on black jeans and combat boots. As his hair dries, it starts to fly away with static.

"Why? You want to come?"

"Me? I couldn't."

I couldn't? It's not like I haven't done it. Maybe this is exactly what I need right now. Maybe this is some sort of ticket out of this rut. A ticket to a place that I forgot about when I was with Peter.

He heads back to the bathroom, and sings along with the music. He didn't answer my question, but what do I care anyway?

He runs into the living room and jumps up on the coffee table that's actually a big old dusty trunk and dances around while lip-syncing the lyrics to the song.

"There's a smile, my lovely Genesis. I knew I could get one out of you."

"I smile."

"Not too much."

That's what Rose says too. That I don't have to be so tough all the time. Not to think so much about everything. It's a hard thing to let go of. So I let my mouth curl up. Like I'm testing my own smile to make sure it works. And I feel lighter. Like I want to jump into this air current that Seth floats around in.

"I smile."

"I know you do. I can tell."

"You can?"

"We did spend a little time together last night, you know?"

"I wish I could remember."

"You ever performed before? Acting? Music? Whatever?"

"Yeah, I've been in some plays."

"I knew it!"

"How did you know?"

"I didn't, really. I was acting."

"Oh."

"You should come tomorrow."

"I can't."

He squeezes in closer to me on the couch than should be allowed. Then he takes my face into his hands, like he's examining my skin and eyes. His face gets so close to mine that I can smell the mint on his freshly brushed teeth, and then he drops it. "Confirmed. You're a living, breathing human being. Which is exactly what they are looking for in this play."

"Come on."

"I can tell you're considering it."

"No, I'm not."

"Look, this is how I see it. Two people meet randomly on a roof ledge one night. A roof ledge! So, do they jump off together or do they just retreat back into their holes?"

A roof ledge was the perfect place to meet this guy.

"And then you left your phone here, and then I just happen to be going to an audition. Too many coincidences. I can tell you're a jumper. Not a retreater."

I look at the dead phone in my hands.

"What's the play?"

"Fuck if I know."

"Seriously?"

"I told you, I'm throwing caution to the wind. I'm taking the jump. I don't need something established. I want something totally off the wall. Totally off the beaten track."

"I don't think it's such a good idea."

"Well, don't decide now. But if you're still thinking about it when you wake up tomorrow, you should just go for it."

Something deep and buried inside myself is starting to scratch its way out. What am I so afraid of?

"If you're not thinking about it, then we can just forget anything ever happened. Deal?"

I'm smiling again. Like he's turned me upside down.

"Deal."

ACT II
SCENE 2

(This scene takes place in Genesis's
living room. Lights rise to GENESIS
reading on the couch. There is a knock
on the door. She isn't expecting anyone,
but when she looks out the window to see
who it is, she doesn't seem surprised.
She starts to sneak out of the room, but
another knock makes her think twice.)

PETER
(Speaking through the door)
      Gen! I know you're home.

(She opens the door. PETER moves toward
her, and she doesn't react. He puts his
arms around her. She lets him but
doesn't move. She's rigid, unresponsive.)

                    PETER
         Genny Penny.

(They continue to embrace, and PETER
kisses her head and ad libs sweet,
soothing words until she finally
moves her arms around him too. When
they separate, we can see that
GENESIS has been crying into his
shoulder.)

                    PETER
              I was afraid to come here.
              Afraid you wouldn't answer
              the door. Afraid you
              wouldn't let me touch you.
              You disappeared, Gen.
              Where were you?

                    GENESIS
              It's been really hard
              around here.

                    PETER
         You've missed the whole
         week of school.

                    GENESIS
         I know.

PETER
And you haven't responded
to any of my calls or
texts.

GENESIS
My mom has needed me.
There's been a lot to take
care of this week. It's a
lot to put on someone
else.

PETER
You shouldn't have to do
everything.

GENESIS
No, I mean I don't want to
put any of it on you.

PETER
I'm supposed to be your
boyfriend, Genesis.

GENESIS
I know.

PETER
You have to let me in.
Whatever it is. I can
handle it. I'm not going

anywhere. I'm not going to
leave you.

                    GENESIS
I know.

                    PETER
I think I can handle a lot
more than you give me
credit for.

                    GENESIS
Everything is so perfect
for you. Believe me, you
don't want to see what
happens around here
sometimes.

                    PETER
Is that what you think?
That everything for me is
perfect?

                    GENESIS
Isn't it?

                    PETER
Seems we have a lot to
learn about each other.
Both ways.

                    GENESIS
        I'd take strict parents
        and threats of grounding
        and total support and
        encouragement over a dead
        dad and a mom who was too
        scared to be alone all
        week.

                    PETER
        I love you, Genesis.

                    GENESIS
        What?

                    PETER
        I do. I love you. Let me
        in. Let me be here for
        you.
(She nods.)
        You want rules? Here's one:
        Don't ignore my calls. You
        have to respond to me.

                    GENESIS
        And if I don't?

                    PETER
        Then you're grounded.

                    GENESIS
        I wanted to respond.

PETER
I thought you were gone. I
should have come sooner.

GENESIS
I do too.

PETER
I'm not psychic.

GENESIS
No, I mean. I do too. Love
you.

(PETER embraces her again. They kiss.)

PETER
I love you.

GENESIS
I can let you in. I just
hope you're ready.

PETER
Let's do this. Let's jump
in. No retreating. Only
jumping. One . . .
two . . . three . . .

(Blackout.)

CONTINUE YOUR NORMAL ROUTINE WHEN READY

As we're heading into the station, we hear the train coming, and Seth flies down the stairs. I chase after him, and we're through the closing doors just in time.

We take two seats next to each other, and I can see our blurred reflection in the window across the way. Seth taps his toes and drums against the metal pole in front of us. He points out a man wearing one orange sock and one polka-dotted, while another man, weathered and tired, plays a familiar tune on his harmonica.

"I have an idea," Seth says suddenly. "How about I skip my first class, and we go get something to eat?"

I search for every excuse not to go with Seth. Must plug in phone. Must call Rose. What else was on my list?

"We'll get off at Third Avenue. One of my favorite spots is near there. What do you say, Genesis Johnson?"

I don't know. I don't know. I don't know. Part of me is already in his current, but part of me wants to just push forward, go home, carry on with my plan.

"Don't answer. We've still got the river between Brooklyn and Manhattan to travel through," he says. "That's underwater. But don't worry, you can still breathe."

I may be able to breathe, but before I can exhale, an automated voice tells us we've made it to First Avenue. Getting closer. I watch the light behind our reflections streak and flash.

One more stop to decide. No time for a pros and cons list. No time to weigh one thing against the other. I just shouldn't go. I can stay on this train and transfer at Eighth Avenue to make it up to Port Authority. Don't I have things to do?

Then I hear the voice again on the speakers. "This is Third Avenue. The next stop will be Union Square."

We're here.

I stand.

Seth's off.

Another, more authoritative, voice takes over. "Stand clear of the closing doors, please."

I'm still on the train.

A warning bell chimes, and the doors start to close.

Seth faces me. His expression doesn't change. I look for encouragement or annoyance or something that could propel me in either direction, but he's left me here on the ledge to make my own decision, and the doors are literally closing in front of my face.

But then I slip through and let them close behind me. I hear the train screech and squeal, and the world spins in front of my face. I blink and see Seth with his hand raised.

"Right on," he says with his hand still in the air. "Come on, don't leave me hanging here."

Oh, a high five. I press my hand into his and hold it there. He grabs it and leads me up the stairs, out into the city.

We wind through the streets of the East Village. It's an unusually warm day for winter. We still need our coats and scarves, but the sun is bright. We walk to St. Mark's Place, where the sidewalks are cluttered with bright-framed sunglasses and feather boas, striped stockings and wallet chains. We pass a place called Bowery Poetry Club, and I imagine Delilah at the microphone, zigzagging her way into the audience's hearts.

"Are you sure you don't have to go to class?"

"Don't worry about that. Shouldn't you be in school yourself, young lady?"

"Long story."

We aren't far from the Planned Parenthood. Half a mile, I would guess. Maybe less. So much can happen in the span of three days. The world can lurch and halt, then spin in the other direction, apparently.

"Do you like ramen?"

Truthfully, the only ramen I've ever eaten comes dried in a pouch with a spice pack in foil, but somehow I don't think that's what he means.

"I think so."

"There's no better time for ramen than a winter afternoon. Especially after a night of drinking. Trust me."

He opens a door for me, and we duck into a storefront with

fogged-up windows, taking two seats at the counter. The walls are peeling white paint and sweating. My face instantly fills with heat. There is no music playing.

Seth orders us two bowls of miso ramen and a pot of tea. There is one other person in the restaurant sitting at a table in the corner. Postcards with varying levels of light damage cover one wall. Anywhere from Kentucky to Tahiti.

He props his elbows on the counter and leans sideways to face me. I look straight ahead to the cooks in the kitchen.

"So," he says. "Tell me everything."

"Everything?"

"Everything."

"What do you want to know?"

"I already told you. Everything!"

Everything sounds like more than I can stomach right now.

"You can start with the long story about why you're not in school today, if you want."

"The short answer? I'm suspended."

"Oh, wow! A bad girl. No wonder I like you."

He likes me? This is not good. Someone in the kitchen rings a bell. I watch our server carry a steaming bowl to the man in the corner doing a crossword puzzle in a newspaper. He tucks the pen behind his ear and folds up the paper.

"I'm really not, though."

"I know. I know. So why are you suspended, then?"

The story that leads up to the suspension pricks at my tongue, but I haven't had a chance to make any sense of the order of events. What am I doing here, having lunch with another guy? What am I doing here when I have so much to figure out? "Can we talk about something else, actually?"

"Anything you want," he says, and unzips his hoodie. It is getting warmer in here the longer we sit. "What are you thinking about right now?"

"I'm thinking about how I don't know how I got here."

"That's easy. The L train."

"You know what I mean."

His mouth is edible when he smiles.

"My parents used to live in this neighborhood."

"Where?"

I don't answer. I wish I knew more about their life here. I know they had an apartment on East Seventh and Avenue D. I know they had to walk up three flights to get into it. I know they covered their ceiling with twinkle lights and one wall was painted like a cow. There aren't many pictures. Just a scattering of stories.

"My dad wrote plays."

"It's in your blood, then."

"I guess it is."

I try to ignore the feeling that my dad is watching me now because that seems so corny, but yeah, it kind of feels like that. Kind of like he sent this guide to take me here, to the place he once found inspiration. I feel him sometimes. His spirit. I never told Peter that. Never told anyone that.

But then I look at Seth and he's just a guy. That's it. A stranger, really. And maybe he's here to take me somewhere, but he wasn't sent from the worlds beyond. "I haven't acted since he died."

"Oh, I'm so sorry."

I fold my hands in my lap.

"How did he die?"

I haven't been faced with this choice in a long time—to tell the truth or the *story*. Everyone in my world already knows how he died (thank you, Vanessa!), but this is the first time a stranger has come to this crossroads. His eyes are locked into me.

"Heroin."

"Whoa."

"Yeah."

We let those words settle between us. The server drops two bowls of ramen on the counter. There are slices of pork and half a soft-boiled egg, and scallions and kernels of corn swimming in the bowl. Seth doesn't touch his. He waits for me to continue.

"I stopped doing any theater because I didn't want to look into the audience and not see him there."

"What did you do instead?"

"I guess I fell in love."

I press my spoon into the bowl, and the contents swirl around each other. I fill it up with broth and sip the warm saltiness.

"Are you still in love?"

"I don't think so."

Seth opens his package of chopsticks, rubs them together, and picks up his half egg first.

"Have *you* ever been in love?" I ask him.

He rests his chopsticks across the ledge of the bowl. "Yes, I have."

"Have you ever had your heart broken?"

"Completely crushed."

We stop and look at each other again. It's easy to open up to him, and I'm not exactly sure why.

"So," he says. "Is your heart broken?"

"I guess it is."

"And it'll heal in three weeks?"

"Three weeks? Oh. Well, part of me will."

"Okay."

I decide to try the noodles now, and there is no graceful approach. I manage to get a bite off the chopsticks before the rest slips into the bowl and splashes both of us. He laughs and asks the server for forks.

"I'm not too proud to use a fork."

My skin feels cracked open. My heart seems to have pushed itself outside of my body right now. We slurp our soup.

"Why do you want to do a play away from school?"

"That's complicated."

"Try me."

Seth shakes hot sauce into his bowl and then hands it to me. I splash a couple drops into the bowl and watch the red streak through the broth.

"Okay, so I'm in my second year now, right?"

"Okay."

"And last year, it just all seemed too easy."

"How so?"

"Like, within the walls of NYU, there's definitely competition, but it doesn't feel real to me. It doesn't feel like there's any kind of struggle behind what we're making there."

"And you want the struggle?"

"I think I might."

"Why isn't there a struggle there?"

"I'm not exactly sure. Maybe because everyone has money from their parents or something. Too much security."

"Do you?"

"I do."

"Where are you from?"

"Indiana. The Hoosier State," he says, laughing.

"What's a Hoosier?"

"I'm a Hoosier!"

"Okay."

I wonder if I pried too much. But then I remember what I just shared.

"Do you ever want to move here?" he asks.

"To New York?"

"Yeah."

"I'm not sure."

"No?"

"I'm not sure of much of anything right now."

"Are you sure that you're eating the most delicious bowl of ramen you've ever had?"

"That I am sure of."

"Bringing you back to life?"

"Thankfully, yes. I really did it to myself last night."

He smiles and drinks the last of his broth from the bowl.

"I am very sad to report that I have to head to my next class. This one I can't miss." Seth pays for our lunch and we bundle back up. The man has returned to his crossword puzzle. He nods good-bye to us.

"Can I walk you to class?"

Seth holds out his elbow, and I latch on.

As we walk, he tells me about moving to New York, and how he never would have come here if he hadn't caught his girlfriend cheating on him. He was going to stay and they were going to move to Indianapolis together. But then he caught her and that pushed him enough to get out to New York and leave it all behind.

We stop in front of a building with a purple flag flying, across the street from Washington Square Park.

"Come to the audition tomorrow. There's a reason why our paths crossed last night."

"I don't know if I'm ready."

"I don't know if you are either, but sometimes you have to take a leap and find out." He looks at his phone. "Shit. I'm so sorry. I have to run."

"Go. It's fine."

He takes my jaw in his hands and moves his face toward mine. I know where he's going, and I want to stop him, but I'm not sure I'm strong enough. His breath hits my skin. "Are you sure I can't kiss you?"

"No."

"No, you're not sure?"

"I'm not sure. But I think not right now."

His forehead lands on mine. "Fair enough. Text me and I'll send you the details for tomorrow. Anyone can come. You don't need to prepare anything."

He pinches my nose and shows me his thumb between his fingers. "Plus, I'm taking this, and you might want it back."

I smile the kind of smile that zaps your insides. Fizzle, sizzle, pop. And watch him walk into the building.

Then I turn and stare across the park. Delilah's building is just on the other side. The building that was my refuge two days ago now casts a giant shadow right into my gut.

About-face.

ACT II
SCENE 3

(This scene takes place in the kitchen.
Music plays faintly in the background.
At rise, GENESIS sets the table. MOM
sits curled into her chair at the head.
Offstage, we hear the sounds of people
coming into the house, and DELILAH and
AUNT KAYLA enter carrying bags of
food.)

                    AUNT KAYLA
          Happy Thanksgiving, honey.

(She hugs GENESIS. So does DELILAH.
Then greets MOM before unpacking the
food.)

                   AUNT KAYLA
I wanted to cook, ladies,
but it was just too
tempting to order
everything.

                   DELILAH
That's fine, Mom. Everything
looks delicious.

                   AUNT KAYLA
Is that okay, Genny? I
wanted this to be as
normal as possible.

                   GENESIS
It's fine. I'm not sure
she'll eat.

                   AUNT KAYLA
Mary, how you feeling?

                   GENESIS
She hasn't said anything
today. But she's at the
table, so that's good.

                   AUNT KAYLA
Mary, I know you love
Thanksgiving. I got the
yams with the marshmallows.

You're the only person in
this universe who likes
that dish.

                GENESIS
My dad liked it.

(Everyone looks at MOM. She doesn't
really move.)

                AUNT KAYLA
You're right. Devon did
like it. You guys and your
sweet teeth. Are you
hungry?

                GENESIS
Kind of.

                AUNT KAYLA
Is this okay?

                DELILAH
Mom, stop worrying. Let's
eat. Right, Aunt Mary?

(She still doesn't move.)

                    GENESIS
          Believe me, getting her to
          the table is progress.
          Don't worry. I'll make her
          eat when you guys leave.

                    AUNT KAYLA
          Mary, I'm glad you're here
          at this table with us. I'm
          thankful for it. Dev would
          have been happy to see you
          at the table with us too.

                    GENESIS
          It's weird Ally isn't here.

(AUNT KAYLA nods.)

                    GENESIS
          They're doing dinner at
          their house. We were
          invited.

                    AUNT KAYLA
          I know. They invited us
          too. Thoughtful, really.
          All things considered.

                    GENESIS
          You talk to them?

                    AUNT KAYLA
Of course I do.

                    GENESIS
Oh.

(AUNT KAYLA dishes up food on
everyone's plates.)

                    GENESIS
Did Gran say if she was
ever going to come by? To
see us?

                    AUNT KAYLA
No, hon.

                    GENESIS
Okay.

                    AUNT KAYLA
I can take you to see them
if you want.

                    GENESIS
I don't know.

                    AUNT KAYLA
Up to you.

                    GENESIS
          I know.

(Food is served.)

                    AUNT KAYLA
(Joking)
          Should we say grace?

                    DELILAH
          Good food, good meat, good
          God, let's eat!

                    AUNT KAYLA
          Such an irreverent child.

                    DELILAH
          You lucked out.

                    AUNT KAYLA
          I sure did. So, are you
          going to tell them, Delly?

                    GENESIS
          Tell us what?

                    AUNT KAYLA
          Can I?

DELILAH
I will. I sent in my
application to NYU.

GENESIS
That's awesome! Why didn't
you text me?

DELILAH
I did. I texted you to call
me. That I had some news.

GENESIS
Oh. Right. You did text me
that.

AUNT KAYLA
It's been a hard week,
hasn't it?

GENESIS
I'm sorry, Del.

DELILAH
I understand. Don't worry
about it.

GENESIS
Will you keep me posted?

                    DELILAH
          I will. But I'll spare you
          the details. You don't
          want in on my anxiety hell.
          I'm already checking the
          mailbox every hour, and
          they probably haven't even
          opened my package yet.

                    GENESIS
          They'll mail the answer?

                    AUNT KAYLA
          They'll probably e-mail.
          Or call.

                    GENESIS
          You're leaving me in
          Jersey?

                    DELILAH
          It's not far.

                    AUNT KAYLA
          I do wish you'd send in
          something to Rutgers too.

                    DELILAH
          I have to be in New York.

(MOM coughs.)

              AUNT KAYLA
I know. I wish my brother
could have taken you there
to see the school.

(Silence)

(MOM gets up and floats out.)

              AUNT KAYLA
I'm sorry, Gen.

              GENESIS
It's okay. I'll check on
her in a minute.

              AUNT KAYLA
We're not supposed to stop
talking about him.

              GENESIS
I know.

              AUNT KAYLA
Let me go. You stay put.

              GENESIS
Okay.

(AUNT KAYLA fills up a bowl with yams.)

                    AUNT KAYLA
          I'm taking these.

                    GENESIS
          Good plan.

(She exits.)

                    DELILAH
          Are you okay?

                    GENESIS
          Actually, I am.

                    DELILAH
          My mom talks about him
          even more at home.

                    GENESIS
          It is really okay.

                    DELILAH
          I'm just checking on you.

                    GENESIS
          I know. I actually have
          something I want to tell
          you.

                    DELILAH
          Oh yeah?

GENESIS
Yeah.

DELILAH
Oh my God. That smile on
your face. What is going
on?

GENESIS
Well . . . okay, I'll just
say it. . . . I'm in love.

DELILAH
No shit.

GENESIS
It's the strangest time
for it to happen.

DELILAH
Do I know him?

GENESIS
I don't think so. Peter
Sage?

DELILAH
Peter Sage. Nope. I don't.
Well, I can't wait to meet
him.

> GENESIS
> You will.

> DELILAH
> He better treat you right
> or he'll have your cousin
> to answer to!

> GENESIS
> I know that. And that's
> what I love about you.

> DELILAH
> Seriously. I know you have
> Rose, and I know my mom is
> all up in your business,
> but I'm here for you too.
> Anything you need.

> GENESIS
> I know that too.

> DELILAH
> Does he know everything?

> GENESIS
> Not yet.

> DELILAH
> He can handle it?

GENESIS
I'm pretty sure he can.

(GENESIS looks toward her mother's
room. DELILAH keeps eating.)

(Lights fade.)

YOU ARE
NOT ALONE

Rose's car is parked in front of my house when I get back home.
I should have expected it. When she doesn't get an answer, she
shows up. I'm not even to the porch yet when the door swings
open and she stands silhouetted, ready to unleash.

"Where have you been?"

Good question. Where have I been? I close my eyes and the
almost-kisses of this afternoon flutter in my chest.

"It's nearly eight o'clock, and I haven't heard from you
all day."

I hold up my phone. "It's dead."

"Which is exactly what I thought you were. Dead. Jesus,

Gen, you can't act like you did last night and then not respond to anyone."

"Rose, my phone is dead. Let me plug it in, and then we'll play catch-up, okay?"

She follows me into my room.

"At ease, soldier. I'm home. I'm not going anywhere."

I plug the phone in and drop into my bed. She gets in with me, and lets me take a few breaths. Last night's story. I have to face it now.

"Did I fuck up really bad last night?"

She shakes her head, but the kind that means yes. Then my phone starts buzzing out of control. "As I'm sure you can imagine, I've texted you about eighty times."

I do have thirty-seven text messages: twenty-one from Rose, nine from Delilah, four from Ally, three from Gran.

Zero from Peter.

"I can't go through this now. Can you just tell me what happened last night?"

"Have you talked to Delilah today?" Rose asks.

"Rose, I'm just getting to my phone for the first time today. I left it at that guy's house last night and went to get it."

"That guy? You went to see that guy today?"

"So?"

"Oh, Gen, you need to talk to Delilah."

"Why?"

"You need to talk to Delly, Gen. She's not very happy with you right now."

"What?"

Whowhatwherewhenwhyhow?

"I guess she knows him."

"Yeah, so? And is he, like, an ax-murderer or something? Because to me he seems like a really sweet guy."

She looks at me like I've gone insane. And really, I don't know why I'm defending him. He actually could be an ax-murderer, for all I know.

"He's not an ax-murderer. But she does know someone who dated him."

"So?"

"So, what?"

"Does she like him or something?"

"Are you kidding me?"

"No, I'm not kidding."

"Genesis, is your head really that far up your ass?"

"What are you talking about?"

"It's not always about you!" She raises her voice so much that I'm sure my mom can hear us now. Hopefully today she doesn't want to get involved.

"I'm not saying it is!"

"You don't have to say it, Genesis. It just always is. You never notice anything Delilah does for you. Or anyone."

We're both on our feet now. She is right in my face.

"You should talk about being self-centered! You're the most self-centered person I know!" I spit back, my heart accelerating.

"Then you haven't looked at yourself in a long time. You think no one will ever understand you. But NEWS FLASH! WE DO! Stop pushing everyone away like you did Peter."

I stop.

Drop.

She doesn't back away.

"Is that what you think, Rose? That it was my fault that he left me AT FUCKING PLANNED PARENTHOOD?"

Now not just my mom hears this, but all of Point Shelley.

"Genesis. Please."

"Why would you say something like that?"

"I'm sorry."

"Is that what people are saying? Is that what people think? That I pushed him away? That it's all my fault?"

"I don't think that, Gen."

"Then why did you say that?"

"Just stop. Sometimes you don't look at the full picture. Don't forget some of the conversations we started having. About getting bored. About not knowing if you were actually right for each other."

She's right.

And even though I want to shove her out the door and be alone right now, I resist. I pull myself together.

"What happened last night?" I ask.

"What do you remember?"

"Not a whole lot."

"Delilah was worried about you when she went to Kendra's apartment and you weren't there. Not because this dude is an ax-murderer. Not because she likes him. But because she didn't want you to do something stupid you might regret. Maybe she went overboard. Maybe it was an overreaction. But she was worried."

"I was just having a good time."

"Gen, you were black-out drunk. The whole drive home we had to keep pulling over so you could puke out of the car."

"Really?"

She nods. "Really."

"Oh my God."

"Yeah."

"And how did you find me?"

"She found out which apartment was his, and went pounding on the door. Will wanted to beat him up, but that's because he's an idiot."

"I'm afraid to ask what was going on when you found us."

"You were passed out in his bed. He was swearing up and down he didn't do anything to you. That you begged him to take you up to his apartment so you could go to sleep. He said he kept asking you if he should tell someone and you said it didn't matter. So he took your word for it. I felt sort of bad for him. The way Delilah and Will were acting, it was kind of like they thought he was a rapist or something."

My heart picks up again. "He is *not* a rapist! That is crazy!"

"Calm down, calm down. I don't think so either. I know you get sleepy when you drink. We should have been paying better attention."

"He didn't do anything to me!"

"Genesis! I'm not saying he did. I'm just saying what happened."

I accept this.

"So then we tried to wake you up but you were fighting us. Delilah was being so mean to that guy. I wanted to stick up for him, but I also just wanted to get you home."

"This is awful. I can't believe he didn't say anything to me about all of this."

"If I were that dude I'd want to steer clear of you and Delilah for a while. I'm surprised you saw each other today."

"I guess I am too. Wow. I really can't remember any of this."

"You were pounding drinks. All you wanted to do last night was forget."

I can't believe this story. I can't believe he wanted to see me today. Much less skip class and have lunch with me.

"Rose, I think I need to be alone."

"Not yet, Gen. I'm not going home yet. You can't keep running away."

And I know I can't. But sometimes running away is actually running toward something, right? Toward something I need. I get back into bed, and when Rose goes to the bathroom, I dig up Seth's number and send this: *I don't need until morning to decide.*

He responds right away: *I didn't think you would.*

Him: *Meet in the city beforehand?*

Me: *Okay. Yes.*

Him: *Are you sure???????????*

Me: *So sure.*

Him: *Can't wait.*

(Me: melting.)

(Him: someone who is not Peter.)

(Me: smiling because I can't help it.)

Rose sees me with the phone and asks if I'm texting Delilah. Right here, right now, I like that the part of last night with all the drama *isn't* in my brain. I like that I erased it all. Texting Delilah means un-erasing. It means conversations. It means explaining myself and my actions.

"Who the hell are you texting, if not Delilah?"

"Oh, Rose," I say. "Free pass, please. This one needs to wait until morning."

"It's that guy, isn't it?"

"Free pass, Rose."

She doesn't like it, but free passes are always honored in our friendship. She crawls back into bed with me.

"I slept with Will last night," she says. "After we got you into bed."

I spring up.

"Here?"

She laughs. "No! My parents are out of town."

"Your parents are always out of town."

"That's all you have to say?"

"No. I just don't know if I can handle thinking about you and Will naked together."

"I'll just tell you one thing."

"Okay, go ahead," I say, burying my head in anticipation.

"It was . . . amazing."

I peek out from under the covers, and swear the stars are reflecting in her eyes.

ACT II
SCENE 4

(This scene takes place in a bedroom.
Lights rise to GENESIS and PETER making
out on her bed. Music plays, something
dark and romantic. Things heat up and
GENESIS pushes too far. PETER jumps out
of bed and turns off the stereo.)

                    PETER
          Gen. I can't.

(She doesn't move from the bed.)

                    GENESIS
          I know. I know.

(PETER goes back to sit with her. They
share an awkward moment of silence.)

(That continues.)

(And continues.)

(She sits up.)

> PETER
> I just . . .

> GENESIS
> I know. Marriage.

> PETER
> I know it's old-fashioned.
> But it's always been
> important to me.

> GENESIS
> Let's get married, then.

(They laugh.)

> GENESIS
> We probably will. Don't
> you think?

> PETER
> Probably.

> GENESIS
> I can't imagine being with
> anyone else, can you?

                    PETER
          No, I can't.

                    GENESIS
          There's a math equation
          somewhere in here. See how
          it all adds up?

                    PETER
          I love you.

                    GENESIS
          Then kiss me.

(He does.)

                    GENESIS
          Don't stop. Don't ever
          stop.

(Blackout.)

IF YOUR TEMPERATURE REACHES 100.4°, CALL US IMMEDIATELY

I meet Seth on the corner of East Fourteenth Street and First Avenue the next day, and I'm proud of myself for getting so good at navigating the city. I haven't slowed down enough today to stop and question this decision. I didn't tell Rose. I set up dinner with the grandparents and sister for seven o'clock, which should be plenty of time to do this and get home.

When I see him, it takes everything inside me not to jump up and wrap myself around him. We lock into a long, warm hug. Separating feels like peeling off layers of staticky laundry. We barely talk as we head down First Avenue. Maybe he's nervous. Maybe he's preparing himself. I haven't done this in so long, I don't even know how to prepare myself.

He leads me to a bar, not a theater. It smells like stale booze, and my stomach quivers again with the reminder of the other night. I've never seen a bar in the daytime before. Not that I've seen many at night either. The space is drenched in red. Red furniture. Red neon signs. Red curtains. Like we're in an old-fashioned den or speakeasy. A place that swallows light and spits out dust.

A kind of freakishly tall lady wearing all gray, with burning, bright red hair, hands out paperwork. But even with the heat from her hair, I feel cold around her. Her gaze is hard. Her expression is unforgiving. A bald man wearing mismatched plaid and round, vintage spectacles sits in the corner, concentrating, and scanning with an intense, scrutinizing gaze. My first instinct is to duck into the opposite corner. Out of sight.

There are more people here than I expected. Everyone in the room is a little tattered, a little frayed around the edges. I see another teenage-looking girl in the room and relax a little. I sit next to Seth on a black chair with a ripped vinyl seat cushion and start filling out the audition form.

Name.

That's easy.

Address.

Hmm. Should I put that I live in New Jersey? I guess it doesn't matter, but I feel weird about it for some reason. Like there would be a prejudice or something. So I lie and put down the address for Planned Parenthood. Is that weird? I can only think of two New York addresses right now—that, and Delilah's. And I don't want to put an NYU address. Seth seems to want to separate himself from the school, so I do too.

More statistical questions follow: e-mail, phone number, etc. And I fill those out accordingly.

Height.

Also easy, five foot eight.

Weight.

Geez, that's a little personal, isn't it? But okay. I weighed one twenty-five at the clinic when I was pregnant. Too skinny, the nurse told me. I bet I weigh less now. A lot has left my body since then.

Age.

I've got to put another lie in here. I peek over at Seth's form to see if he's put nineteen or twenty-one. He covers his paper like I'm trying to cheat off a test, and then laughs.

"What's the matter?" he says.

"Just wondering about age."

He opens up his hand. Twenty-two. I shake my head and put nineteen on my own sheet.

He laughs again, but nods his approval.

Voice type.

Singing? Alto. Like Mom.

Attach CV or write down your past three productions.

Shit.

It's been so long, surely that can't look good. Can I fill in a space for the past few years that says:

Grieving father's death.

Too dramatic?

What about:

Rejected past until it snuck back up on me one drunken night in Brooklyn.

I could put the show at Point Shelley Community Theater. With the chicken-bone death-scene director. I can't remember his last name, though. And it was so long ago and in New Jersey. I could put the productions I did at school after that. But that's high school, and I don't think I should call any attention to that. I think I'll just leave it blank.

Formal training?

Shit again. Why am I here exactly? Will they see right through this? Okay, I did take piano lessons. I put down *classical piano.* This doesn't bode so well for me, I think.

Then there's this:

PLEASE LIST ALL CONFLICTS YOU HAVE BETWEEN NOW AND THE PERFORMANCE DATES AND WHETHER THEY ARE FLEXIBLE OR NOT.

I look over the schedule. All the rehearsals are at night, so that's good. Maybe I don't have to tell them I go to high school during the day. High school. That totally happened today, and I am totally suspended. Peter was there. And he knows I'm suspended. And I haven't been in Advanced Writing to see if he and Vanessa will now sit with each other like we used to. I look around the room again. It's full of people scratching out their forms. There aren't any more chairs, so some people sit on the splintered black floor. I see a few people have finished and returned their forms to the fire-headed lady.

I write down I have a daytime conflict on weekdays up until the performance date, but that it's flexible. It is, right? If they really needed me. I don't want to be *in*flexible.

Then it hits me that I really want to do this.

I want in on this scene. It may be fraying and tattered, but it's charged. I get that itching feeling again that my dad is somehow responsible for this afternoon, but shake it off.

The form asks me if I'd be interested in any other aspect

of this production if I'm not cast: stage crew, lighting, sound, set construction, makeup, ushering, advertising, tickets/concessions. I don't want to seem ridiculous, so I just check *stage crew* and *set construction*. Even though I'm pretty sure I'd do whatever they wanted me to. Not that I have any experience with any of it. Then I check *makeup*. Just for fun.

Fire Lady collects the forms from people who haven't already turned them in. Some people have headshots. Seth does, but he tells me not to worry. I see not everyone has them. The other teenager does. She tries to smile at me, but I ignore her. I don't know why. Fire Lady tells me to stand, and gestures toward another guy across the room to do the same, then gives us a piece of paper with a scene to prepare. Sides, they're called. I look to Seth, who gestures for me to move. Peter would never believe it if he could see me here now.

Seth's the type of guy Mrs. Sage would call a *hoodlum* because his hair is long. Or this guy about to read a scene with me—he has a tattoo of a dagger on his forearm in thick black ink. I don't think *hoodlum* would be a strong enough word for Mrs. Sage.

"Hi, I'm Toby," my hoodlum scene partner says.

"Genesis."

"I guess you're reading Ruby."

"That makes sense."

"And I'm Felix."

"Do you know what this play is about?"

"Love. What else? And sex. And violence. That's all I really know. But Casper Maguire is a fucking genius."

"That's the bald guy?"

"You don't know him?"

I shake my head.

"Where have you been?"

"Uhhh . . . New Jersey?"

Toby laughs. I wasn't actually trying to be funny. And I realize I shouldn't have said that, since apparently I live at Planned Parenthood.

We run through the scene four times before we're called to the area marked as the stage. In the faint light slipping out from under the black-curtained window, there's the trace of a dried puddle of liquid. I press my toe into it, and it sticks. Red lights shine into our eyes.

"You are in hell," Casper (apparently, the Great) says.

Casper is a head floating in smoke. Like the powerful Wizard of Oz when he's all big and green and loud. Only, Casper whispers. I haven't seen Casper speak to anyone since I entered this room, except Fire Lady. Ms. Karen would call his behavior *brooding*. She says I do it too. She says sometimes I should just smile and it might change my mood.

"Excuse me?" I say.

"Ruby. She is, you are, in hell in this scene. You are completely ruined. You just lost the only man you ever loved. Can you imagine that?"

I swallow hard. And nod.

He nods back. I look down to make sure my feet are firmly on the ground. They are. And that's not because they are stuck to dried liquor. I have to think. I have to understand what's behind these words I'm about to say for anyone to care. For anyone to feel anything. I close my eyes and think about that while I breathe in and out. In. Out.

"Whenever you're ready," Casper says gently. But also sort of growling. Gentle growling.

I look up to see Toby standing patiently. I'm really an actor right now, and it fills me with electricity. I raise my head and he starts.

"Ruby, it's too late. It's like we've already died and we're ghosts now."

Then Toby, I mean Felix, turns into Peter before me, and I stop for a second. I stop, then remember the words, the answers, are on the paper in my shaking hands. I blink, hard.

"So why can't we be ghosts, then? I'd be anything to stay with you. Anything. Here, take my heart. Take my skin. Take my hair. I don't need any of it if I'm not with you. Take me back, Felix. I don't want to be alive if you walk out that door. I don't care about anything else. I don't care. I don't care. I don't care I don't care I don't . . ."

Then Toby/Felix/Peter is holding me by my upper arms as I let my weight drop. I could cry, but I'm fighting it. Because I know that's what Ruby would do. At least in this moment. And I only just met her.

The rest of the scene flies. I fight against the man who's leaving me. I rip myself open and I bleed.

When we get to the end of the lines, we're both panting.

I click back into myself, into this red room. With the bald man scribbling notes into a notepad smaller than his palm.

Toby and I look at each other. Then back to Casper Maguire, who closes his notepad and sets it on the chair next to him.

"You stay up there," Casper says, pointing to Toby. Then to me: "You are done."

"Done?" I say, struggling because I think all the breath has left my body.

"Done." Then he's calling another girl up to read with Toby.

Fire Lady stops me to make sure she has my phone number

down correctly, then tells me they will post the cast list tomorrow afternoon in front of the bar, or I can wait for the call. I look around for Seth. But he is deep into his scene practice, and I decide to slip away without saying good-bye. Maybe I won't even come back to check the cast list. Maybe I won't answer my phone. Maybe I imagined too hard that I belong here, and I'm just a dumb girl from New Jersey who needs to play with kids her own age.

Slipping away doesn't work. Seth is in front of me like magic.

"Where you going?" he asks.

"They said I was done. I think I blew it."

"Blew it? No way, Gen. I saw you up there. That was . . ."

I don't let him finish. "Well, he doesn't want to see any more, so I'm done."

"Will you wait for me?"

I look to the door. My escape. Then to a clock on the wall. It's just about six now. Shit. My grandparents and sister will be at my house in an hour. If I leave now, I'll only be a little bit late.

"Come on. I'll be done soon. Wait for me. You have something better to do?"

Um.

Something better to do?

It's hard to believe any place but right here exists. It's hard to imagine there are people expecting me at home, even though I know it's true.

"Don't go."

Maybe Casper will look my way one last time and remember me. Maybe I'm still auditioning by sitting here and waiting. Seth's partner calls him back.

Ms. Karen would call this justifying. Fine. I'm justifying. But I'm also letting go. I start to text my family but I'm interrupted by Seth's voice and his audition piece. I turn to watch. He's paired with a tall girl with long, wavy black hair and a slight accent I can't place. Her lips are bright red and so is her sweater. He squeezes her cheeks together in his hand, pushing her lips out like a fish; tilting her head back in a way I'm sure will snap her neck. She bends backward, looking frightened. A couple of tears appear in the corners of her eyes.

"You will never understand how much I love you," he whispers into her mouth. So close to her I can barely hear him. His voice like a hiss. Then he lets go and she drops to her knees.

"Please," she begs. "Please don't leave me."

I haven't had a chance to beg Peter yet. He hasn't given me that. Seth spits on the floor.

Casper stops them.

How could he? It was just getting good.

Everything stalls. We are caught in this moment of loss for the couple onstage.

And then Seth breaks. His face morphs back into itself or out of itself or something supernatural, because I swear he wasn't Seth just a moment ago.

"Thanks so much for the opportunity," he says to Casper.

Shit. I didn't thank anyone.

"Yes. Next please," Casper snarls.

Seth shrugs, and then gathers his things. Fire Lady checks his phone number too and then we're outside again. He's howling into the air.

"That was amazing!" He hollers and laughs and scoops me up to spin me around. "Let's run!"

"Run?"

"Yeah! Let's run! Have you ever run through a crowded New York City sidewalk? It's the best!"

I don't have time to think, time to question, time to doubt.

We're running. Running toward something.

Anything.

Nothing.

Everything.

The world around us blurs into streaks of gray and lights as we run. The city floats up into the blue-black-orange of dusk. When Seth stops abruptly, I run straight into his arms. Just when it can't seem any more like I'm in a movie or a play or a dream.

I look into his face. I can see his breath. Even if I wanted to, I wouldn't be able to detach from his hold. We're just here, letting the vaporized city around us solidify into frozen buildings and sidewalks and trees.

"I'm *not* going to kiss you," he says, and his voice is all breath and ice.

"Okay," I say.

"No protest?"

I don't know how to protest. I don't even know where I am. I don't even know if I'm made of flesh and bone or air and dust.

I put my head down into his chest and breathe in. Lemon soap. Laundry. Smoke.

"I need to go home," I say.

He doesn't protest. Maybe he forgot how to as well.

We walk to the train without touching each other even though it would be so natural to put my hand into his. I'm trying to remember what Peter's hands feel like. I'm sure he held mine on the way into the clinic. Didn't he? I can't remember.

I look over to Seth, who also seems to be deep in thought. The air hovers heavily around us.

At the station entrance, he takes both my hands.

"I'll call you," he says with a half-smile. "Okay?"

I nod and say okay.

"Good."

"I'd like that."

"Good."

"We find out tomorrow."

"Yes, we do."

"Bye, Seth." He lets me go. "Thank you so much."

"You did it yourself."

He blows me a kiss, and I walk down the stairs. When I reach the bottom and look back up into the light of the outside world, he's gone.

ACT II
SCENE 5

(This scene takes place in a church. At
rise, PETER and GENESIS follow MR. and
MRS. SAGE and JIMMY down an aisle, but
at a good distance.)

PETER
You really didn't have to
come.

GENESIS
I wanted to.

PETER
It means a lot to my mom.

                    GENESIS
          Does it mean a lot to you?

                     PETER
          Yes.

                    GENESIS
          That's what I care about.

                     PETER
          She's not all bad, you
          know.

                    GENESIS
          I know that.

                     PETER
          Give it time. She'll let
          you in.

(They sit down. Take out hymnals. Music
starts and the choir sings. GENESIS
watches PETER as he sings along. Her
eyes well up and he takes her hand.)

                    PASTOR
          God grant me the serenity
          To accept the things I
          cannot change;

Courage to change the
things I can;

And wisdom to know the
difference.

(Blackout.)

A PERIOD OF EMOTIONAL PARALYSIS CAN OCCUR

On the bus ride home, all the post-audition elation twists and turns itself into knots. I am not the person I said I was. If they knew my real age, would they think I was just a kid? Not take me seriously? I haven't felt like a kid in so long. I haven't felt like a kid since my dad died. Before that, really. When he'd disappear and my mom would need me *not* to be a kid. She didn't know what to do with kids. Ally was the kid. I was some limbo age. I was the one who did the grocery shopping and wheeled our food home in a granny cart. I was the one who washed our clothes and our sheets and made sure Mom kept her prescriptions filled.

I've always been in that limbo. But I couldn't take care of my mom and another kid. And when my mom ended up in the hospital that day and we had to assure everyone she didn't try to kill herself, that the doctors gave her a bad combination, that no heart could take what she had been prescribed, well, we were just too broken to hold on to Ally anymore. The grandparents took her. And I kept washing our socks and signing the checks to the utility companies.

She didn't try to kill herself.

Grandma was insistent.

I don't want to go home right now. Going home is going backward. If I don't stay on this wave, I'm afraid I'll sink to the bottom of the ocean.

I know the right thing to do would be to text everyone and let them know I'm on my way. But something is stopping me from even pulling my phone out of my bag. Ms. Karen will have a lot to say about this. More justifying. More detachment. But what about just holding on to what feels good? What about pushing forward with all your might?

Why did I leave Seth? Was it really the night before last that we met? It had to have been years, oceans, universes ago. Maybe that's why I can't remember.

And then: an image. Spitting. Spitting vodka like a fountain out of his window and laughing so hard and pushing a pile of clothes off the bed, and then tumbling into it with him and wrapping myself up in him.

There's a piece of the night that somehow I dug up out of the murky mush of my brain.

I hold on to that memory and toss it around for a minute. I can feel it in my teeth.

Then I remember something else. Ease. Comfort. Something inexplicable and undefinable. Something playful and dreamy.

I can't do this. I can't do this. I can't fall. I can't fall into something when I'm so lost, or at least I think I'm supposed to be lost. I'm supposed to fall down at Peter's feet and beg him to take me back. That's what I wanted mere hours ago. Didn't I?

Were we holding hands?

At what point in time did I really lose him?

I'm back at Walmart again like I was just days ago. I'm late and I haven't texted and I have a good long, cold walk ahead of me to get back home. I put my head down and push through it. If the world in New York City felt like vapor, this one feels like stone.

```
                  ACT II
                 SCENE 6

(This scene takes place in a
crowded high school hallway.
Students whisper and point at GENESIS
as she walks through them all. The
mood is dreamlike and the action
choreographed to music. She grows
more confused and more afraid,
which we see on her face. Until she
meets PETER. They take each other's
hands.)


                 GENESIS
       What is this? Where am I?


                  PETER
       They know, Genesis.
       Someone told.
```

> GENESIS
> About what?

> PETER
> Your dad.

> GENESIS
> What do they care?

> PETER
> People like gossip. Try to
> ignore them.

> GENESIS
> They're not making it
> easy.

> PETER
> I've got you.

> GENESIS
> How the hell did they find
> out? Did you tell anyone?

> PETER
> No. I would never.

> GENESIS
> No?

> PETER
> You know that.

GENESIS
Only a few people know.
This doesn't make any
sense.

(The swarm around them grows again,
music rises until they are offstage.)

(Cut music abruptly with blackout.)

ALLOW SOME EXTRA
TIME AT HOME TO REST

This play takes place in a house. A house full of people waiting for you. A house full of people waiting even though no one usually is. This house full of people could be worried, could be angry, could be fed up with your selfishness.

On a normal day, you wouldn't have gone to New York City and let yourself get swept up in someone else's whirlwind.

On a normal day, you'd be home to check on your mom and make sure she's functioning like a human being.

Okay, and by *you,* I mean me. I have to take some responsibility here. I have to accept the things I cannot change, or whatever that prayer was I heard in church. The Serenity Prayer. But what is that, really? Who says we can't change the things we can't accept?

Here I am, Genesis Johnson, the serene star of my own fucked-up drama, and they're all waiting for my entrance.

I missed my entrance, so they've had to improvise.

This is NOT what will happen:

Gran: *Genesis, it's so good to see you! You look so happy and healthy!*

Mom: *Genesis, I feel well enough for your sister to come back home and live with us!*

Ally: *Genesis, you are the best big sister in the whole world!*

Okay, that play never existed anyway. But I don't know what waits for me in there. I don't think I'll get grounded or anything, but leaving my mom alone with her parents for that long is really a cluster of dynamite waiting to blow up.

I can't see through the frosted windows of my house. The orange porch light flickers as if saying: *proceed with caution.*

I open the front door. It's unlocked. I half expect to be blown over by a tornado or for a tidal wave of water to flood over me. Too late to save anyone but myself!

Or maybe it's a house full of ice sculptures, each in an aggravated pose, eternally about to tap their toes in impatience.

But instead there's music? And laughter? Warmth?

Cast of characters:

Grandma Pauline

Grandpa Joe

Sister Ally

Mother Mary (yeah, I know)

They sit around the kitchen table, each holding a hand of cards. The counter is covered with empty Chinese food containers, and the sink is full of dishes. My mother and grand-father have full glasses of wine.

They look like a family.

And somehow this image is more shocking than anything my wild imagination could have produced.

In fact, they don't even notice I've walked in, and I watch Ally make a move that causes my mother to throw her hand of cards down on the table and my grandma to mess up Ally's hair lovingly. She wiggles away, and then notices me.

"Gen!" she squeals, and runs over to me.

Then things shift, tighten up.

"Well, look who has finally graced us with her presence," Gran says.

"Nice of you to show up for your own party," says my grandpa.

I look at my mom, whose smile has faded, and I get that old familiar feeling that I'm the source of her sadness.

Everything would have been different without me.

But she stands up and joins our hug.

I'm in an embrace with my mother and sister.

And there is no better feeling in the world.

I think about Peter. How he would be grounded for behavior like this, and somehow in my alternate reality, it brings my family together.

My not being here to moderate could have led to explosions, but somehow didn't.

"Your mother convinced me not to call the police," says Gran.

"The police?"

"You are two hours late and your phone goes straight to voice mail. Yes, the police."

"A person has to be missing for forty-eight hours before they do anything," says my sister.

"Yes, Ally."

"I was convinced you were kidnapped and held at gunpoint to make that phone call to us, inviting us over into some crazy-dangerous situation," she says.

"You've been watching too many crime shows," says Gran.

"I watch forensic shows."

"Our little scientist."

This is a weird play.

"It's why I always wear glitter."

I look at Ally and see her eyelids are, indeed, covered in glitter.

"I gave up that fight," says Gran. "She's expressing herself, I'm told."

"I don't get it," I say.

"Well," says Ally, "if I'm ever the victim of a crime, this glitter will transfer to the perpetrator as trace evidence. And he might not take as much care washing it off as he would, say, blood."

"Ally!" my mom exclaims.

"Oh, yes, this is what we have on our hands lately."

"Is this because you live in the city now? Are you scared?" my mom asks.

"No. The glitter just looks really good, don't you think?"

She twirls around and I want to laugh, but also I hate that she might feel scared.

"No one is going to hurt you," says my grandmother.

No one will hurt us. This is the most bullshit advice adults ever give. There's so much that will hurt us; it's how we take care of ourselves afterward that matters. The aftercare. I can't tell Ally about all the hurt I've been through in the past seventy-two hours, but I do know she knows the same deep and brutal hurt I do, the one that left the nasty, corrugated scar. We got the same wound.

I kind of love that her defense mechanism is glitter anyway. Maybe I should invest in some glitter so no one can hurt me. Or if they do, at least they'll get caught.

"See, look at Gen. There's a little from the hug. Turn your face."

I do and I guess the trace glitter catches the light.

"Now she's marked."

"All right, little miss detective, why don't you find out where your sister has been for the past two hours?"

Ally pulls a notebook from her back pocket, pure Harriet the Spy.

"Fact: Genesis returned to the scene of the crime at nine p.m. Two hours late."

"Scene of the crime?"

"Well, so to speak."

So to speak? When did my little sister grow up?

"Fact: missing person was uncontactable. Is that a word?"

No one answers her.

"Uncontactable."

"Am I on trial?" I say.

"You're not on trial," my mom chimes in. "I've already explained to my mother that we operate with trust in this house."

"And not common courtesy, it seems."

Oh no. Here we go, dropping the land mines. Will anyone step on one, is the question.

"I'm sorry. I really am. I lost track of time. That's it."

"Where were you?"

"No trial," says my mom.

But the questions begin anyway:

Where were you?

Why didn't you call?

Why did you invite us over if you weren't going to be here?

How are you handling the home life right now?

And then:

Are you on drugs?

Record screech.

"Excuse me, what did you ask?"

I look at Ally, who is practically eating her hand she's digging so hard into her nails.

"Given your father's history, I have to ask," says Gran. "We're concerned about your erratic behavior."

"Erratic behavior?"

"Do you think the school doesn't call us when you get in trouble?"

I had never thought of that, to be honest. I'm not usually in trouble. I tell my grandparents what grades I get on my report cards, but I didn't know they were in on the day-to-day.

"And the credit card charge to New Jersey Transit? Two days in a row? Where were you going?"

The trial continues.

"Did you know she was suspended, Mary?"

My mother doesn't answer. She scratches her arms and looks toward the door out of here.

"We just see now that we should have asked you sooner, Mary."

"Asked me what?" my mom asks her mother.

"If you were using drugs. We knew he was. We suspected you were too. We should have helped."

"I'm going to bed."

I don't know these stories. No one ever tells me. I've had to figure everything out myself. And it's felt like screaming underwater for years in this house. Why is my mom waking up now? I want to scream at her not to go to bed now that she's finally here and present. Can she be here? Can we keep Ally? What can we do now? Don't go hide. Don't go to bed. Change the things you can't accept.

But who am I to talk? I could have been here two hours earlier.

"That's fine. We're leaving."

"We are?" Ally asks.

"Yes."

"Why didn't Daddy ask someone for help?" Ally says. "Why was he so selfish?"

I want to shake her. I want to rip her away from the grandparents and anything they might be telling her. Any skewed image they might be painting of him. I want her to remember the road trips to Maryland and the horses on the beach. I want her to remember how he always had a cigarette tucked behind his ear, but we never saw him smoking. I want her to remember his plays. I want her to remember singing songs like "Who Put the Bomp" and "The Flying Purple People Eater" while dancing around in the kitchen. I don't want her to only remember he was a junkie who left his family behind.

"He tried, honey," my mom says. "Sometimes no one listens."

I don't want Ally to only think about what it was like when he would leave and we didn't know when he'd be back. Even though, of course, she'll always remember the time he didn't and wouldn't *ever* make it back.

"We could have, right? Why weren't we enough?"

"We were, sweetheart."

Grandparents and Ally exit stage right. Mom and I sit in silence. Waiting for someone to write the next scene.

(Doorbell rings.)

We look at each other. Are they back?

When I open the door, the person standing there is my former best friend and boyfriend stealer, VANESSA.

ACT II
SCENE 7

(This scene takes place in Ms. Karen's
office.)

          MS. KAREN
    So, there's absolutely
    nothing you want to speak
    with me about today?
(GENESIS shakes her head.)
    No one acting strangely
    toward you? No unusual
    behavior?
(GENESIS shakes her head again.)
    I don't know why you're
    shutting me out today.

(No response.)
>Okay, we're not talking
>today.

(No response. MS. KAREN stands up and
paces around while she talks. GENESIS
remains motionless and silent.)
>I'll tell you what I know.
>Is that okay?

(No response.)
>I know you didn't tell me
>everything before.

(No response.)
>I know I'm not deaf.
>
>I know people are talking
>about you.
>
>I know when a person is
>the center of all this
>talking, it is hurtful,
>and I know it's not your
>fault.

(GENESIS turns away.)
>I know you loved your dad
>very much, and it doesn't
>matter how he died, just
>that he's not with you
>anymore.
>
>I know losing a parent is
>one of the hardest things
>a person ever goes through.

I know people talk before
they know the whole story.

I know they will never
know how you feel.

I know that drug addiction
is more common in this
community than people talk
about.

I know that you are not
the only person in this
school who has had to deal
with this kind of thing.

I know that heroin use in
particular can be one of
those secret, silent
addictions.

I know that there are many
more people using the drug
than we can keep track of.

I know that it wasn't your
responsibility to keep
track of him, Genesis.

Did you hear me? It wasn't.

GENESIS
If you know so much, do
you know who told?

MS. KAREN
I do.

GENESIS
You do?

MS. KAREN
I was told in confidence.

GENESIS
Well, it obviously is not
in confidence anymore
because the whole school
is talking about me. I
didn't know this actually
happened. I always thought
people were being dramatic
when they said "the whole
school is talking about
you." It's actually fucking
possible, though. Who told?

MS. KAREN
I know that your knowing
the answer to that
question won't change
anything.

GENESIS
Are you kidding? It will
change everything!

MS. KAREN
I'm glad you're talking to
me now.

GENESIS
Please tell me it wasn't
Peter.

MS. KAREN
Would you like to talk
about your relationship
with Peter?

GENESIS
No.

MS. KAREN
Do you have any reason
to believe Peter would
give up information like
this?

GENESIS
No.

MS. KAREN
The person who told was
only concerned about you.

                    GENESIS
Bullshit.

               MS. KAREN
Genesis.

                    GENESIS
It is. Whoever told wasn't
concerned for me or they
would have kept their
mouth shut.

               MS. KAREN
Why didn't you tell me?

                    GENESIS
Because it's none of your
business.

               MS. KAREN
Genesis.

                    GENESIS
Who was it?

               MS. KAREN
I don't think having that
information will help you
at all.

                    GENESIS
It's KILLING me.

                    MS. KAREN
          Who do you think it was?

                    GENESIS
          Will you tell me if I'm
          right?

                    MS. KAREN
          (Sighing)
          Let's move on, Genesis.

                    GENESIS
          Peter?

                    MS. KAREN
          You said you didn't think
          it was him.

                    GENESIS
          Someone in my family?

                    MS. KAREN
          Let's focus on the real
          issue here.

                    GENESIS
          Was it Will?

                    MS. KAREN
          Did Will Fontaine know?

                    GENESIS
          Our mothers are, like,
          best friends. Why did you
          answer that time?

                    MS. KAREN
          I didn't.

                    GENESIS
          Vanessa?

                    MS. KAREN
          Genesis, you need to calm
          down. You need to redirect
          this energy.

                    GENESIS
          It had to have been
          Vanessa. I will never
          forgive her for this.

          (GENESIS runs out of the room, leaving
          MS. KAREN practically spinning in her
          chair.)

          (Blackout.)

ARE YOU EXPERIENCING
ANY REGRET?

"What are you doing here, Vanessa?"

Now it's my turn to ask questions. Prosecute. I'm taking charge of the script.

Except I don't really know what I want to ask her. It's been so long since we've actually talked. I step out onto the porch, and close the door behind us. Moisture seeps into my socks.

"I was a real bitch in the bathroom," she says.

Okay, she can start.

"I wanted you to think I was with Peter. I admit it."

I flinch at the sound of his name from her mouth.

"I don't know where everything went wrong with us."

Why is Vanessa saying what I wish Peter would say to me?

"I can see you're getting upset. Can we talk about this? About everything? I know you have more to get out. I forgive you for attacking me."

I still don't know what to say.

"I guess that's how you guys deal with things here in this house, right? Just shut it all in?"

"Why would you say that?"

"She speaks!"

I hold on to my hands so tight, they tingle. I just nod at her and try to think about the cold. And the wind blowing around her on the porch.

"Vanessa, you need to go."

"Yeah, I shouldn't have come. I don't know what to say to you. You clearly hate me. I don't understand."

"Oh, you don't understand?" I snap back at her. "You don't understand why I might not want to be friends with someone who systematically dismantled our friendship so that she could get her hands on my boyfriend? Was that your plan when you told everyone about my dad?"

"What are you talking about?"

"I figured it out. I figured out why you told."

"I'm not following."

"You told about my dad overdosing so Mrs. Sage wouldn't approve of the relationship. So she'd have something real to hold on to. A real reason to hate me. She would never let her son be with a girl who comes from a family like mine, right? A perfect way to break us up."

"Are you even listening to me?"

"What?"

"He doesn't want me. He never did. He never will. I've hated you for so long for getting the only thing I wanted. The only thing I'm guilty of is being jealous. And today I acted stupid. I wanted you to know what it felt like when I found out about you guys. Remember that? In the library? My heart exploded that day. And you knew it. You knew it."

Vanessa is crying.

"I didn't dismantle our friendship, Genesis! You ditched me when Rose came around," Vanessa says. "And Genesis, I told because I was worried about you. I told because they asked me why you were missing so much school. They called me in. They acted like they already knew. I was scared shitless. And I was mostly scared for you. That's it."

I'm silent.

We look at each other, or the space between us, I'm not sure which, and I say, "Why did you say we'd never make it anyway?"

"You and Peter?"

"Obviously."

"Do you think you will?"

I *did* think. I totally did think we'd make it. I never thought about life with anyone else but him.

"You know he loves you."

Do I? Does love mean disappearing?

"He hasn't jumped into another relationship. With me. With anyone. He mostly seems confused right now. And a little lost. Which is so not Peter."

"Do you know why we broke up?" I have no idea why I'm asking this right now. Except as a hope for a small release. Of pressure. Of everything.

"I mean, it seems like you just grew apart."

I shake my head.

"It was something more?"

"It was."

"Do you want to tell me?"

I shake my head. But I kind of do. But I know I can't. It wouldn't be fair to him.

"You don't have to. But you can."

She touches my shoulder, and I look down at our feet.

"That's really why you told?"

She drops her hand, and turns to walk down the path without answering. I cross my arms, and watch Vanessa shrink away.

When I get back in the house, my mom has moved onto the couch in the living room.

"Are you okay, Mom?"

She shows me her saddest smile. One that means so many things. She is the master of the sad smile.

"You've had to deal with so much, Gen."

"I've done all right, though, haven't I?"

"You've done more than all right. You don't need me."

"I don't like it when you talk like that."

"It's true. You've been taking perfectly good care of yourself since . . ." She pastes the sad smile back on her face instead of finishing her sentence.

"Will you tell me if you need anything, Mom?"

"You shouldn't have to ask that of me. That's what I should be asking you."

I've dreamed of this conversation. I swear I have. I swear I've had the dream that my mom says that exact thing, and all of a sudden my dad is back and Ally is here, and we're operating like a goddamn normal family with real smiles that come from love, not from pain.

And then I have to ask her: "Do you ever . . . feel him? Like, feel him here?"

Her eyes fill up, and her face drops.

I listen to her breathing.

She doesn't answer.

I kiss her forehead and smell where her hair meets her skin. Oil of Olay sunscreen face lotion and Pantene two-in-one. She's smelled like these two things for as long as I can remember. I could pick these scents out of a blind smell test, I know it.

"One day things will be normal, right?" I ask her.

"I'm working on it."

I nod so I won't cry, and head to my room.

I text Rose to tell her about Vanessa. She immediately calls, but I send it to voice mail.

Me: *Can we talk in the morning?*

Rose: *I'll come over.*

Me: *Sounds perfect.*

Rose: *Are you okay?*

Everyone always wants to know if I'm okay. I just don't know.

I just don't know.

But somehow the world keeps spinning. Spinning spinning spinning.

ACT II
SCENE 8

(This scene takes place in the Morning
Thunder Café, again. Focus is on
GENESIS and ROSE in a booth.)

                    ROSE
          I can't believe it! I can't
          believe it! You popped
          Peter Sage's cherry! It's
          an earthly miracle!

                    GENESIS
          Shhhh! Rose! Shut up!

                    ROSE
          I can't! You've just shaken
          the entire moral order of
          the world to its core.

You've just ripped poor
Peter Sage from the Garden
of Eden. You are Point
Shelley's Eve. You
are . . .

                    GENESIS
          Rose, please. Relax.

                    ROSE
          Holy shit! You lost your
          virginity too!

                    GENESIS
          Do you want to hear about
          this or what?

(SERVER comes by with cheese fries and
Cokes.)

                    ROSE
          Yes! Every detail!

                    GENESIS
          It was perfect.

                    ROSE
          Oh God. Of course it was.

                    GENESIS
          He got keys to Cal's
          family beach house.

>   ROSE
> I might throw up.

>   GENESIS
> Candles and everything.
> We were, like, playing
> house all weekend. Cooking
> and sitting by the fire and
> well, you know . . .

>   ROSE
> Did you do it more than
> once?

>   GENESIS
> So many times!

(They laugh.)

>   ROSE
> That's my girl.
(Beat)
> What did your mom do all
> weekend?

>   GENESIS
> Aunt Kayla came over.
(They eat.)
> I love him, Rose.

                    ROSE
I know you do. It's cute.
Disgusting too. But cute.

                  GENESIS
I think we're going to be
together forever.

                    ROSE
That's because you're a
girl who just got laid all
weekend. We'll see.

                  GENESIS
We'll see. But I could feel
it, you know? Kind of like
it was our house in the
future. And that's what it
will be like with us.

                    ROSE
I have never heard you
talk like this.

                  GENESIS
I want you to be in love
too.

                    ROSE
Who, me? Bah. I don't
need it.

                    GENESIS
We all do.

                    ROSE
I have you. I don't need a
boyfriend.

                    GENESIS
You'll find it.

                    ROSE
We'll see.

                    GENESIS
We'll see.

(WILL FONTAINE enters and acknowledges
both girls on his way by. ROSE reacts
with disgust. GENESIS is friendly.)

(Lights fade.)

SUPPORT GROUPS
ARE AVAILABLE

The smell of melting butter drifts through the house. I know it's not my mother with butter in a pan, so it must be Rose in the kitchen. Which is slightly frightening. But when I get there, I see eggs and cheese and herbs, and bread sitting in the toaster, ready to be pushed in.

"What's all this?"

She spins around from looking at a recipe in her phone.

"I couldn't sleep. I'm dying to hear about Vanessa."

"So you brought breakfast?"

"I decided to make a frittata."

"A what?"

"A frittata. It's like a quiche without crust."

I peek over her shoulder and see a bit of eggshell in the batter. I dip my finger in to get it out.

"You forgot something."

"And he thought he could teach me to crack an egg open with one hand."

"He?"

Rose blushes. When she does, I wipe the shell piece onto her nose, then duck under her swat.

"Let me show you what I've learned."

"Considering the last time we ate your cooking, it was burnt oatmeal, I'm going to start praying now."

"Peter would be so proud."

And then I sink a little.

"I'm sorry," she says, abandoning the eggy goop and turning off the flame on the stove. "Too soon."

I step backward and steady myself on the counter. "No, it's fine. It's okay."

This is one of those times when *okay* doesn't mean anything but *Let's drop it.*

"Okay."

"Okay."

"Okay, so call me crazy, but I don't know how to use your coffee maker."

"And you're making a crustless quiche?"

"Hey! That's sophisticated technology."

I put the coffee on, and sit at the kitchen table to watch Rose sweat her way through the frittata recipe.

Rose picks another little piece of shell out of her whisked eggs. "So, what about Vanessa last night?"

Here we go. And there isn't even any caffeine in her blood yet.

"Dish."

I tell her about the conversation. About how Vanessa knew about the rumor of their getting together, and even though it wasn't true, she wanted to watch my reaction. Then about how she told the school about my dad and home situation because she was worried about me. Not for any malicious reason. I skip the part about her saying I ditched her for Rose.

"And you believed her?"

"I did. I really did. I almost told her about the abortion too."

"Whoa."

"I know."

"Do you think she wants to be friends again?"

"I can't tell."

"But they're not together."

"No."

Rose pours the coffee into two mugs.

"Are you still feeling sick?"

Am I? Body check. I wasn't spotting when I went to the bathroom, and I actually feel relatively normal. Maybe I'm through it. Maybe my body recovered pretty quickly.

Now for the heart.

"Do you miss him?"

Him. I miss him. I really do. Even with someone starting to fill up the missing space, I still wonder where he is and what he's doing. "Yeah."

Rose puts her frittata in the oven and brings the coffee to the table. I know she wants to ask me about Seth. She circles around it with grace, but I can see the curiosity in her eyes. I wonder if I can dodge the questions. I wonder if I can escape to the city this afternoon without telling her. Not that I won't; I just don't want to yet. I don't want that bubble to burst.

"Gen, what are you doing tonight?"

Busted. "Nothing planned."

"Okay, good."

"Why good?"

"Maybe we can hang out."

"Yeah, maybe."

"If I don't get too preoccupied," she says with a wink.

"Ew, gross. Can I remind you you're talking about Will Fontaine?"

"He's taking me roller skating. That's too ridiculous and cute."

"You are."

As the timer on the oven goes off, Rose gets a text from Will that he wants to meet her early. She looks from her phone to the frittata to me to the phone.

"Oh, Rose, just go."

"But breakfast!"

"Since when do you eat breakfast?"

"True." She gathers her stuff, then comes to hug me good-bye. "Seriously, maybe we can all hang later."

"Yeah, maybe," I say again, knowing that she's just trying to be nice. She'll get caught up in Fontaine-land, and my route to the city (and Seth) will be clear and easy. "Bye, lovebird."

"Shush up," she says, and runs out the door.

My phone buzzes.

Seth: *Results today!*

All this back and forth to the city is making me a little bit dizzy. And *results* makes it sound so medical. I haven't much liked any of the results I've discovered lately. Especially the two pink lines. But these are results for an audition. I auditioned for an off-Broadway show yesterday. Isn't that what happened?

Seth: *Meet me earlier and go together?*
Genesis: *Okay. Where?*
Seth: *Coffee shop on Bowery and 2nd. Forget the name. 4pm?*
Genesis: *See you there.*

I peek into my mom's room. She's reading.

"There's frittata that Rose made, and coffee in the pot."

"Thanks."

"You okay?"

Mom nods. "Love you, Gen Gen."

She hasn't called me that in forever. We look at each other, but I know the conversation isn't going any further. We're not going to talk about last night. We're not going to talk about how I broke up with my boyfriend and had an abortion and tried out for a play in the city. I won't tell her that sometimes if you open yourself up a little bit, someone else might surprise you, even boys with shaggy hair and gigantic smiles, so instead I just say:

"Love you too."

Across the aisle from me on the bus, a man has fallen asleep with his mouth open, holding his glasses against his chest. I can see the silver fillings in the backs of his teeth. Cool air trickles through the window, into the overheated vessel.

I almost text Delilah, but just can't bring myself to.

We reach Port Authority, and the castaway passengers stir. Rose told me once when she went to Puerto Rico everyone cheered when they landed. These droopy people in the bus from coastal New Jersey don't seem too thrilled to reach Manhattan. No cheering.

By the time I navigate Port Authority and the subway system to the coffee shop where Seth wants to meet, it's 3:37 p.m.

Just a little bit early. The sky is overcast, a cool gray blanket over the city. People seem to move extra slowly today. Like the air is thick and hard to break through.

I order an Earl Grey tea before Seth gets there, and add milk and honey. The first sip burns my tongue, making my mouth all fuzzy. I let the tea sit, and look through my phone to pass the time. Delilah's texts from Wednesday start with a very simple *looking for u* and then progress to *FUCKING ANSWER ME!*

I put the phone down next to the tea that is too hot to drink. My dad told me when I was a kid that one day he'd take me to Paris. That I wouldn't believe the food and the people and the music and the underground theater. I was always confused by that word, *underground*, and I imagined a group of people who burrowed into the ground and made worlds full of music and all the people's skin turned green like they were in a Toulouse-Lautrec painting.

Now I guess I'm on my way to an underground theater. Though it's upstairs at a bar.

It's 3:54 p.m. The door chimes every time it opens, but so far no Seth. I wonder if he's nervous. I wonder what will happen if he makes it in and I don't. Or the other way around. I try to imagine what it will be like to come into the city at night with all the green underground people and make a play with them. I wonder what Casper is like as a director. I wonder why everyone says he's so crazy when at the audition he barely even spoke. Just watched from the shadows. And dismissed people too quickly. And probably never noticed me because I'm just a kid trying to sneak into their world. Trying to find their portal.

The bell on the door chimes again a few minutes later and

in walks Fire Lady. Today she wears solid turquoise from top to bottom, not the solid gray of yesterday. Her lipstick is bright magenta and she enters the café like a cheetah. I duck down into my seat because I don't really want her to see me. But she is a big cat, and stalks me right away. She doesn't say hello.

"You were at the audition yesterday."

That's not a question. So I don't say anything. But I think I kind of nod. I look at her eyes, which look violet to me. She has a slight German accent. But I might be imagining that.

"You will go to look at the results at five o'clock."

Again, not a question. And again, this word: *results*. I can't help but feel I'm learning how many months I have to live.

Maybe, in a way, that's not so far off.

"Cat got your tongue?"

I'm not kidding. She actually said that. I choke out, "No."

"Good. I have the list here if you want to see it."

Maybe she thinks I should look to save myself the embarrassment of finding out I didn't make it in front of everyone else.

The door chimes again. I look up expecting Seth, but no. Phone says 4:07. He's late.

But now the choice. Do I look? Or do I wait for Seth so we can look together? I'm an impostor. I shouldn't even be doing this. This is his thing, not mine. I should look at the list and get out of here before he arrives. Or actually I shouldn't look. I should just go. Pulse. Pump. Breathe. The answer is right in front of me. Right in her hand. Seth is late. Maybe it's okay to look. I can better prepare myself for his reaction.

But I'm stuck.

Shipwrecked.

And why is my tea still too hot to drink?

"I don't know. I'm waiting for someone."

"Suit yourself," she says, and clicks her tongue. "Genesis Johnson."

She remembers my full name. I look back and forth from my tea to the paper in her hand to the chiming door to my phone to the tea to the paper to the chiming door to my phone.

"How old are you now?"

Shit. What did I say on my form? "Nineteen."

"It hasn't been that much time."

"Excuse me?" Oh no. Did I blow it by lying?

"I remember you."

Well, that's positive, but it was only yesterday so I should hope she would remember me.

"I was at the funeral," she says.

I'm sorry. I'm sorry. What? I've only ever been to one funeral. When I was fifteen.

"I never forget faces," she says to me. "And I watched you that whole day."

A lot of his old friends were there. I kept to myself. There was a great divide between family and old friends. Like opposite sides of the battlefield.

"That's impossible."

"Nothing is impossible, Genesis Johnson. Nothing is coincidence."

She reminds me right now of the Ghost of Christmas Past. Like she will guide me through the Village and show me my parents' life here. Without children.

"You knew my dad?" How could I have randomly walked into this piece of his world? This piece of his secret world? He knows this woman with the fiery hair? How? I try to look at the insides of her arms. To see if she has the marks he used to have. The bruises and holes I never understood. But her sleeves are long.

"Sorry to throw you off. I knew it had to be you yesterday. You didn't know where you were? Who *we* were?"

I shake my head. "No. I came with my friend, Seth."

She nods slowly. "Okay."

That's all she says, then turns to leave. I want to stop her but I don't know what I would stop her for. Answers? Apparently when you start ripping the patches off, more questions flood your way. And this coincidence is too much. This is too much, like I've been guided into this by my dead father, and I don't believe in that kind of thing. Would Peter say this is God? He tried to explain God to me and I never got it. I never felt it.

Now it's 4:23 p.m. and still no Seth.

Maybe I should have looked. Then I wouldn't have to face that woman again. I could just go back home and not worry about Seth and not worry about the curveballs I seem to constantly be thrown.

Chime.

Not Seth.

Then my phone vibrates.

Seth: *So sorry! L train sux. Walking from train. Meet at theater?*

I take a sip of the tea. Perfect and creamy. Finally.

I text back: *See you there.*

ACT II
SCENE 9

(This scene takes place in Peter's
bedroom. Lights rise to GENESIS and
PETER in bed, under the covers and not
clothed.)

                    PETER
          I'm going to marry you
          someday, Genesis Johnson.

                    GENESIS
          Make an honest woman out
          of me?

                    PETER
          That could be tricky.

GENESIS
Oh, stop.

PETER
I really love you. I love
this.

GENESIS
That's because we're
having sex now.

PETER
No, I'm serious. I never
knew it could feel like
this.

GENESIS
My point exactly.

(He pushes her playfully. Then they
have a quiet moment.)

PETER
You're my forever girl.

GENESIS
What does that mean?

PETER
That I'm sure I'm going to
love you forever. You're

going to become the same
thing as forever. My
forever girl.

> GENESIS
> That's so cheesy.

> PETER
> But you like it.

> GENESIS
> Duh.

(They kiss.)

> PETER
> See? You're definitely my
> forever.

> GENESIS
> That's a long time.

> PETER
> Nothing I can't handle.

> GENESIS
> Does your mom like me,
> Peter?

> PETER
> Where did that come from?

                    GENESIS
    I don't know. I feel like
    I'm trying. I went to
    church with you.

                    PETER
    Mom is not the easiest
    person.

                    GENESIS
    You're telling me.

                    PETER
    She just has unshakable
    morals.

                    GENESIS
    And I'm immoral?

                    PETER
    That's a strong word.

                    GENESIS
    She imagined someone
    different for you?

                    PETER
    Gen, I love my mother, but
    she doesn't get to choose
    who I'm with.

                    GENESIS
          She knows about my dad,
          obviously.

                     PETER
          Yes.

                    GENESIS
          And she probably thinks
          I'm a drug addict or
          something.

                     PETER
          She doesn't think you're a
          drug addict.
(Beat)
          You know she works with
          addicts at the Asbury Park
          Hope Center? Well,
          volunteers.

                    GENESIS
          She does?

                     PETER
          Yes.

                    GENESIS
          What does she do there?

                    PETER
Faith-based recovery and
care.

                    GENESIS
Why didn't you ever tell
me this?

                    PETER
I don't know. You never
really asked.

(GENESIS considers this.)

               PETER (CONTINUED)
Believe it or not, she
just wants to help people.

                    GENESIS
Why doesn't she work?

                    PETER
She used to.

                    GENESIS
What did she do?

                    PETER
She was a pediatric nurse.

                    GENESIS
Oh. Why did she stop?

                     PETER
Because she had children.
And my dad made enough to
support the family.

                    GENESIS
Does she know we're having
sex?

                     PETER
No.

                    GENESIS
She probably wishes you
were with someone more
like Vanessa.

                     PETER
Stop it, Gen.

                    GENESIS
We're obviously serious.

                     PETER
Forever is pretty serious.

                    GENESIS
I'm serious.

PETER
Don't forget, you are
corrupting her oldest son.

GENESIS
I'm not doing anything you
don't want to do.

PETER
I know that. And that's
what's most important.

GENESIS
I can't believe you let me
corrupt you in your own
house.

PETER
The coast was clear.

(They start kissing. Sound of a garage
door. PETER jumps out of bed.)

PETER
Shit! Shitshitshitshit.
She's home early.

(GENESIS gathers her clothes. What she
can find, anyway.)

              PETER
Hurry, Genesis. This is
really bad.

              GENESIS
I am. I'm going as fast as
I can.

(But she can't find her shirt. PETER is
freaking out.)

              MRS. SAGE
(Voice approaching)
      Peter? Are you home?

(Panicked faces)

(Blackout.)

RESULTS

Seth sits on the black metal steps leading up to the bar. His face is wrapped in a plaid scarf like a bandit and his hair spills out on either side. He stands when he sees me, and I meet him on the first step. I wonder if I'm supposed to hug him or kiss him on the cheek or what.

I don't do anything.

"It's not up yet." He points to the door.

Toby the Hoodlum shows up next.

"Nervous?" he asks.

Is that what this feeling is? Nerves? I just shrug, and he smiles. My mouth tastes like honey.

Fire Lady appears next—if she's not just a figment of my imagination. Her stare is so strong, I can feel it in my eye sockets. I really do think she can see right into the deepest parts of me. She's seen me in a past life.

Seth looks at her and then to me, as if he's trying to decipher this signal between us, this foreign language.

She takes one step up and lights a thin cigarette.

"What was that?" Seth asks.

"What?"

"The way she just looked at you. Seemed like you were locked in some weird ESP shit there."

"Oh, I ran into her at the coffee shop."

"And?"

I step down onto the sidewalk.

"And she asked if I wanted to know the results."

"AND?"

Seth jumps down to meet me there.

"I said no. That I wanted to wait."

"You are bonkers, girl."

We look up and watch her take a long pull. There is extra smoke with the cold in the air. She smashes the cigarette slowly between two sharpened fingernails and the lit cherry top falls to the metal step. Then she removes that same piece of paper from her bag, tapes it to the door, and walks inside.

Seth doesn't hesitate; he runs up to the door. I don't want to push through the crowd, so I hang back and wait. Just for a moment. Toby gives me a thumbs-up on his way down. I don't know if that is for him or for me.

Seth bounces back toward me, and I try to read his face. "Aren't you going to look?"

What the hell am I doing here? I wonder if it's obvious I'm shaking. The wildest thing is I wasn't even this scared when

I went to the clinic. And I think maybe I should have been. But the fact that Peter isn't here. That he hasn't been in touch. That I'm trying to open myself up right now solidifies that I made the right decision for myself. If he can abandon me so easily when things are difficult, then how were we ever supposed to raise a child anyway? But that's not what is important right now. Right now I have to move one foot in front of the other and read the list and see if I really am turning in a new direction. If I really can move forward on my own.

I'm trying so hard to control my nerves, but even my blood is shaking.

"Go, Genesis. You won't be disappointed. I'm serious."

I walk up the steps to the cast list. This is what it looks like to me:

Gljlkjdsglkj
Lwkejt & GJGJGOJJOSOSJD by FJFJLSL Q Mandojsjdo
Skljdglik   Lskdgjel Wskjdlj
Egvjljl   Fljsdioncklskldfjklhncjskjgfkdjsglvk
Gakjvnjen   Blahblah BLAH
Gjldkdkdk   Qtosofkslfjdkl;lsdk;flsdk;vldksv;kv
mlkcxnm lkcxnlkvnsdlkvlkdjvlkdvslkdnvlknvkzsnvlsndv-
lknsdlknvlskdnvlksndvkldnv mc,mneljivjv

Until I can focus my eyes and make sense of the letters. And I find this:

Gwendolyn   Genesis Johnson

Who is Gwendolyn? I think I say that out loud. Maybe not. Holy shit.

I'm totally cast in this play.

HOLY SHIT.

I'M TOTALLY CAST IN THIS PLAY.

I don't know if I should scream with joy or burst into tears. Seth doesn't wait for me to come back down the steps. He runs up and hugs me.

As I'm smashed up into him he says, "Congratulations, Gwendolyn."

I didn't see his name on there. But I didn't see anything, until my eyes could focus. "Were you? Did you?"

"You're looking at an esteemed member of the ensemble."

"Seth, yes! We did it!"

We did. I did. But how in the hell am I supposed to do this?

"Let's go get some food. I'm starving!" he says.

I'm not hungry in the slightest. But that's okay. I read the note underneath the cast list saying the first read-through of the script is Monday night, 7:30 p.m., at the bar. The first read-through. I see the other teenage-looking girl from the audition. She shrinks a little when she looks, then turns to me.

"What part did you get?"

"Gwendolyn."

"Lucky."

"You?"

She shakes her head.

I still don't know whether to scream or cry. But I'm ready to do all of it.

"I can't believe this. Casper Maguire. Casper fucking Maguire. This is so awesome."

Seth breaks crackers into his lentil soup. I'm looking at my grilled cheese sandwich. He's talking and I'm floating. I still don't know anything about Casper Maguire. I still can't believe what Fire Lady told me. I used to try to imagine what my dad's life was like here. When he'd leave us, I would make myself feel better by imagining this magical place. Now, I'm in it. I'm deep in it. On one hand, I'm kind of flipped out to now have a glimpse into what he was doing over here. On the other hand, whatever he was up to ended up killing him, so there's that.

I wonder if Fire Lady knows my mom.

I really want to tell Peter. Just to see his reaction. But he doesn't deserve to know.

"Thank you, Seth."

"You did the work. You took the leap."

"Seriously, I'm really excited about this."

"Get ready for some serious crazy, my friend."

"I want it."

"Yeah you do."

"I do."

When we finish eating, he says, "Let's celebrate."

As he says this, and as we move to leave the restaurant, my phone starts to ring off the hook. Text after text after text from Rose. I try not to look but they are piling on top of me.

SOS

I need you

Please come here now

I can't believe I'm such an idiot

Why did I ever think I could date Will Fontaine?

HE'S A CHEATING LYING LOSER!!!!

I'm getting all of this while Seth is picking up the tab and then hailing a cab for us.

As soon as we're in the backseat, the phone rings. Rose. I ignore it.

Seth tells the cabdriver his address, but the driver says he doesn't know his way around Brooklyn so we'll have to direct him.

Rose calls incessantly. I keep rejecting, but each time I feel like I'm stabbing her in the heart.

"Looks like someone really wants to get in touch with you."

"Yeah."

"Just answer it. I don't care."

So I do. Which I should have done immediately.

"Where are you?" This is Rose now. On the phone. Her voice is shaky, but still demanding.

"I'm in the city."

"The city? Oh."

"Are you okay?"

"No, I'm not fucking okay and I need my best friend."

"What happened?"

"It's Will."

"What happened?"

"I can't trust anyone, I swear. Once you put out, I swear, everything changes."

"Oh, Rose."

"I need you right now. Please. I don't ask much."

I look over at Seth, who is watching this whole exchange. I don't want to leave him. I know I'm going to have to.

"Are you with Delilah?"

"No."

"Who then?"

"No one."

"Bullshit. It's that guy, isn't it?"

"Maybe."

"Let me talk to him."

"No way, Jose."

"Please. Just for a second."

I must be completely out of my mind because I hand the phone to Seth.

"Hello?... Hi, Rose.... Mmhmm... oh, really?... No, that's fine!... Okay.... Okay.... Okay.... Okay, bye."

He hangs up the phone and hands it to me.

"What? She didn't have anything else to say to me?" I ask.

"No, but she sounds upset. You need to go."

"I know."

"What do you want to do about this cab?"

"I wish you could come with me."

"Do you want me to?"

"Yes."

"Then I will. Driver, to Point Shelley, New Jersey, please."

"Are you out of your mind?"

"Maybe."

"I cannot afford that."

"We'll put it on my credit card. My congratulatory gift to you."

"Some celebration."

"Maybe it will be. I've never been to Point Shelley."

"Rose is going to kill me."

"That sounds like a possibility."

"Let's just go to Port Authority."

The cabdriver is shifting around and trying to interrupt our conversation. "Excuse me? Excuse me? Where are you going? I don't go to New Jersey."

"Please, sir. We're having a family emergency. We have to get there as fast as possible."

They do some negotiating on the price and I sit like an idiot, sweating in my winter coat. I should not accept this gesture. It's too much. And should Seth really have to deal with Rose's drama?

Just stop thinking, Genesis. Just let it happen. Because so far, ever since Peter left, things actually are making a little bit of sense.

In the most senseless of ways.

ACT II
SCENE 10

(This scene takes place at Genesis's
house. We hear sobbing in the darkness.
Lights up to GENESIS and PETER entering
her house, laughing, playful.)

                    PETER
          And then Mr. Villarosa
          couldn't say anything!
          There was no arguing after
          that. Another small
          victory for the common
          people of Point Shelley
          High.

                    GENESIS
          Peter?

          PETER
But Mitch Jennings started
taking his side . . .

          GENESIS
  Peter?

          PETER
  What?

          GENESIS
Do you hear something?

(They stop.)

(Muffled sobbing sounds)

          GENESIS
  Mom?

          PETER
She's not at work?

(GENESIS exits, calling out to her mom.)

    GENESIS (FROM OFFSTAGE)
Mom? Are you in there?
(Pound. Pound. Pound.)
Mom, open the door.

(The sobbing stops. GENESIS rattles the
door and pounds more.)
      Mom, what's wrong? Let me
      in, please. Let me in.
(During this, we watch PETER's
reaction. He doesn't look concerned,
but slightly annoyed, as if he's grown
tired of always dealing with this.)
      Mom?

(Blackout.)

CARRY ON WITH REGULAR ACTIVITIES WHEN READY

You never notice how big the space in the middle of the back-seat of a car is until you want to be closer to the person next to you. I want to fit my head right in that spot between Seth's neck and shoulder, and watch the city lights twinkle across the river. That space is not only a wide river, but a force field I can't penetrate.

But then he scoots over and grabs my hand. Like that space meant nothing. And why should it? I look at our hands together, and sparks shoot through my arm. Through all my bones. Our fingers interlock and his thumb rubs the bottom of my palm, and I want to pull my hand away because it feels so nice, too nice.

"The ride will take a little while, so we may as well get comfortable here, right?" Seth says, and then asks the driver to turn up the classic rock station.

We both stare out the window and watch everything fly by. All I can smell right now is Seth. It surrounds me, holds on to me. Laundry and boy. Boy smell. I love it. I want to eat it. And the music gets louder.

"She seems to have an invisible touch, yeah," he sings into my ear.

"Genesis," I say.

"That's you."

"My namesake," I say, laughing. "You know this song?"

"Of course."

Then we start singing together, "And now it seems I'm falling, falling for her . . ."

My dad used to play this song for me. Another sign? Another smoke signal from the worlds beyond? It's coincidence. They play Genesis on the classic rock station all the time.

Seth closes his eyes when he sings and dances with his fists. I take it all in, through my skin.

When the song ends, a commercial comes on, and the driver turns down the radio.

"What's the best birthday you can remember?" Seth asks me.

I don't know the answer to that question off the top of my head. It would have to be before my dad was gone. I barely remember celebrating after that.

"My first birthday."

"You remember it?"

"No, but I bet it was amazing."

"You avoiding the question?"

"Maybe. Why? What was yours?"

"You want to know?"

I nod.

"I think it was my eighteenth birthday."

"That's mine coming up."

"I know."

And then it hits me. Rose isn't having problems with Will. This is a conspiracy. That must have been what they discussed on the phone and why we're taking a cab all the way to Rose's house.

Seth's teeth fight their way out of his lips and into a smile. He turns, but it's too late. I understand everything.

"You're supposed to be an actor. That's some poker face," I say.

"I don't know what you're talking about."

"How did you know it was my birthday?"

"You told me at my house!"

"Oh, shit." I did. I'm being paranoid. But seriously, this is the way Rose works. She's not having a crisis. "We're going to a surprise party, aren't we?"

"You really want me to tell you?"

"That means yes."

"Yes."

"I can't believe you told me!"

"You figured it out!"

I actually don't know whether to be furious or flattered right now.

"I'd rather know. It's okay."

"Are you sure?"

"Yes. Damn it. Rose! I can't believe I didn't sniff this out sooner. Guess there's been a lot going on."

Seth doesn't respond. He just looks into his folded hands. When did we stop holding hands? I don't remember letting go.

"What was so great about your eighteenth birthday?" I ask him.

"It was the night I decided to move to New York."

"Didn't you make that decision when . . . ?"

"Yep."

The night he discovered his girlfriend was cheating on him.

"It happened on your birthday?"

"Yes, it did."

"And that was your best?"

"Well, it got me here, didn't it?"

Then we pull in front of Rose's house.

"Can we go back? Can we turn around and head back to Brooklyn? I'll pay for it."

"Sorry, Charlie. Rose sounded pretty serious. And I think this may be my first test."

Is Delilah here? I haven't spoken to her since the Brooklyn party. But it would be weird if she didn't at least stop by my birthday party.

I think about what Delilah must have been like when she barged into Seth's apartment. I wonder if he was scared.

"Seth, about the other night . . ."

He puts his hand up to my mouth, and those sparks shoot again, down my jaw and into my throat.

"But I wanted to apologize if anyone was acting psycho or . . ."

Then his lips are on my mouth. He's kissing me. I let myself fall into it like it's the easiest place to be. Like we're falling through this cab floor and down into the underground. Where people are green and music is air. I kiss him like there isn't a man sitting in the front seat waiting for us to pay. I kiss him like there isn't a house full of people waiting to yell *Surprise!*

And then when I think that I might just melt into myself, I push his chest gently to move him off of me. We both sit for a second, with all that space between us, only this time it's just inches, and we catch our breath.

"Sorry," he says.

"No" is all I can manage to say.

"I've wanted to do that since you showed up at my door to get your phone."

Fire. Sparks. Magic.

Ignore it.

No, postpone it.

"Do what?" I say, smiling.

"Kiss you like I meant it."

Hold yourself together. Explosions are messy.

"Let's go see about this party," I say.

"It was supposed to be a surprise."

He kisses me again. But this time our lips barely touch and our noses meet and neither of us moves or breathes. The cabdriver clears his throat, and Seth hands him a credit card without moving his nose from mine.

When we're out of the cab, he grabs my hand again. That house in front of us is full of people who have never seen me hold anyone's hand except for Peter's. Instinctively, I look around for his truck, but of course it's not parked anywhere. If this shindig has been planned for more than a week, then he should have probably brought me here.

Do I even know anyone inside those walls?

I haven't rung Rose's doorbell since the first time I went to her house in seventh grade. I'm sure they are all watching through the windows. Waiting in the shadows.

"Just pretend you're walking onto the stage," he says. "You've rehearsed enough. You know the part."

"What part is that?"

"Well, I've never seen it, but I imagine Genesis Johnson will be surprised her friends threw this together for her. I imagine she will feel flattered and will say thank you over and over. She'll hug a bunch of people who will be very happy they managed this surprise. Then she'll exit toward the kitchen and pour herself a drink that is way too strong, and maybe she'll end up passing out in a stranger's bed."

"Will you just pour that drink for me while I'm doing all the hugging?"

"Sure thing. And I know just the stranger's bed for the grand finale."

I can't decide whether to laugh or hang my head in shame. "That's not really me, you know?"

"Neither of us knows each other very well yet, Genesis. Don't worry so much."

I open Rose's front door. There are still bells on it from Christmas. I brace myself for . . .

(Silence)

No one says anything; no one jumps out. I turn on the lights and see an empty living room. I look at Seth, who shrugs and follows me into the kitchen. What the hell is going on? I thought I had this figured out.

"What is this?" I ask him.

"Beats me."

Are we too late? Did Rose plan a surprise party for me and no one came?

"Rose?" I call out. I can't take it.

She walks into the kitchen with black makeup pooling under her eyes.

"Gen. Finally."

"Rose?"

Her eyes are also red and puffy, and maybe I am an asshole if she really is upset right now. But no. I'm so confused.

"What's going on, Rose?"

She pushes herself into my arms, headfirst. I look at Seth over her head, who shrugs again.

Then there's an eruption of screams, and even though I was expecting it, I jump and pull Rose down onto the floor with me.

She's laughing hysterically as she rolls away. Meanwhile the masses of voices who just yelled *Surprise!* approach slowly, and I want to cover my head and sink into the floor.

"Stand up, Genesis. Happy fucking birthday."

I see Will. I see Anjali. I see Stevie. I see all the people we sit with at lunch. There is one missing face, but I guess I'm getting used to that.

"I knew you'd figure it out," Rose says.

"I almost didn't!"

"Well, I knew you would at some point, because you always do. So I thought this extra layer of surprise would be funny. Like you think you're so smart and then there's actually not a party."

I stand and hug her. "Thanks, Rose."

"You're welcome, Gen. Let's have some fun," she says, slipping a birthday tiara onto my head.

Seth hands me a red Solo cup filled with ice and something pink. I drink it too fast.

"Slow down there, Gen," Rose says. "This party is for you. You have to be here for at least part of it."

"Fine."

"You can crash here too. I told your mom about it."

"I guess Will isn't a cheating, lying loser?"

"Nope."

I squeeze Seth's elbow.

Someone turns music on in the living room, which draws part of the kitchen crowd out. Will winds his way over to us. He's wearing a backward baseball cap and a hoodie with a skateboarding skeleton on it.

"What's up, dude," he says, and nods toward Seth.

Seth holds out his hand. I remember Rose said Will wanted to beat him up when they found me in his apartment. I watch, hoping Will just grabs his hand back.

"I'm Seth. Nice to meet you."

They shake hands. I put my drink down.

"Yeah, buddy. Sorry about the other night. I was just looking out for my girl's friend, you know?"

"I'm not your girl," Rose says, behind this new, uncharacteristic blush.

"Whatever. You will be."

"I'm not your girl's friend," I say.

"Now, that's true. Gen's more like my sister."

I need to change the subject here. "Did you invite Delilah, Rose?"

She shifts a little, but doesn't answer.

"Did you?"

"I did, Gen. I'm not sure if she's coming."

"Not sure or she's definitely not?"

"Not sure. Seriously. Have you talked?"

I shake my head. Then I pick my cup back up and look at the ice melting into the pink liquid.

"She might. You never know."

This is ridiculous. We're not even fighting about anything.

"I have another stupid question," I say to Rose, and pull her away from the boys.

With a fake academic-sounding voice she says, "There are no stupid questions, only stupid answers. Wait, is that how it goes?"

"Does Peter know about this party?" I keep my voice low.

"Of course he does, Gen. This has been planned for weeks."

And now I sip the liquid from my cup. He's not here. He shouldn't be. That would be too confusing. But still. It stings. This was getting planned at the same time our little trip to the city was being planned.

We move into the living room, and a few of my classmates coax me into their dance circle. I humor them. I carry on in my role. I see Seth has no problem chatting it up with strangers. I notice Vanessa isn't here. Not that she should be either. It's just hitting me. These absences. Delilah. Vanessa. Peter.

Seth catches my eye and moves toward me, shaking his hips around and wobbling his knees. He looks like a Claymation figure. We press together, swaying to the music. I can feel people watching, surprised. But I'm made of clay too, fitting myself into a new mold.

Anjali smiles at me, then flips her hair around to the music. Rose and Will join us on the designated dance floor. Rose's party mix is on the stereo. We dance to an old David Bowie song. When he says, "Fashion! Turn to the left!" we all follow. But it's closing in on me. This room, the people. I'm starting to feel the buzz, and like the air in the room is thinning. I excuse myself to the bathroom, extracting myself from the tangle of dancing bodies. Seth starts after me, but I tell him I'll be right back.

"You get your booty back here fast," says Rose. "There's a lot more dancing to do."

I give her a thumbs-up and head up the stairs.

Once I'm in the bathroom, my head starts to spin, and I hold on to the edge of the sink and try to suck in air. The last time I was in here during a party at Rose's house, everything went wrong. With the condom breaking and the laughing and the not caring. If I had been paying attention, maybe I would have noticed Peter did care. That it was really out of his realm to do that sort of thing in a bathroom. I pushed him. I wanted it. I recognize now that he was nervous. I was the one who threw it all to the wind and wanted to get wrapped up in it, who ignored any real problems that might have been going on.

Such as basically hiding the relationship from his mom.

Such as being afraid to be who we really were.

Was it really so bad, though? Bad enough to throw it all away with no conversation, no kiss good-bye?

I can't let myself go there right now. This is my birthday party. I'm here to have fun. With the people who love me and care about me.

I look at myself in the mirror and take off the stupid tiara. I cup my hands and drink water from the sink, wipe my mouth, and walk out the door.

Seth is waiting for me outside.

"You followed me."

He nods.

"Thank you, Seth."

"You gotta stop thanking me."

Then he's kissing me again. I can breathe in this kiss. It's the floating kind, not the falling kind.

"Hey, get a room!" someone yells from downstairs.

"Get down here, Gen!"

I jump onto Seth's back and he hops down the stairs, laughing and almost toppling so many times, yet holding me steady. He starts his silly knee-wobbling dance again, and I beg him to put me down and everyone else laughs and dances, and I'm finally letting myself have fun, finally settling into the ease of having a good time. Just dancing and swaying and kissing and laughing. I've never had such a fun birthday party before.

Then the doorbell rings.

Stevie moves to answer it, with everyone screaming and laughing.

And then, standing in the door frame, plain as day:

Peter.

DO NOT INSERT
ANYTHING

It's one of those scenes. One of those movie scenes. Where the music screeches to a halt and suddenly everyone looks at you. Except the music keeps going, and I jump off Seth's back, and I know I recognize that person in the doorway, and I know it's only been days, but he is a stranger. His face droops over his skull, all sadness, or confusion, or maybe he's aged one hundred years.

I look at Rose, thinking she might intercept. But she's stuck too. We're all stuck.

There is no intercepting.

There is only facing what is right in front of me.

This is an invasion. This isn't fair. He can't just come when he wants to.

He can't.

No one says anything, and I still wish the music would screech itself off. Pop music doesn't quite match the scene. But what idiot is going to turn down the music? It's too obvious.

So I do it.

And then it's quiet.

Seth touches my arm. Everything's askew. He should not be mixed up in this. What is he doing here?

And by *he,* I think I mean both of them.

Peter moves into the living room. He doesn't just look old, he looks scared. His usual confidence sucked out by a room full of people on my side. Though they don't even know why they should be on my side. And why does there have to be sides, anyway?

Should I hate that person standing in front of me?

I can't seem to stir up any hate.

I know it's in me somewhere, but it's not coming out.

Hate would make things so much easier now.

I look at Seth and mouth, *I'm sorry.*

I don't know what I'm sorry for.

I hate this.

I hate all of this.

Then Rose breaks our collective stupor. "Are you kidding me?"

Rose moves forward, Seth backward. There could be an indentation in my flesh where his hand was.

"This isn't the time, Peter," I say, but I also step closer to him.

He reaches out to touch my face, and I shiver from someplace deep, someplace buried, sunken, dead.

"Don't."

Sometimes *don't* means everything but what it's supposed to.

"Gen, I really screwed up."

"No fucking shit you screwed up."

That was Rose. She's not having this. I seem to be swimming through invisible honey.

"What are you doing here? You can't do this. You can't just
show up. That's not how it works."

"Rose, I can handle this," I say.

"So handle it." She turns back to Peter. "What part of your
actions in the past week made you think you were still invited?
Seriously."

"I know. But it's your birthday and . . . Gen."

I'm shaking my head. I'm shaking my head and I want to
close my eyes and make him go away. Here he is, physically, the
actual, physical Peter Sage. My boyfriend? We haven't offi-
cially broken up yet. I mean, with a conversation.

I look at Rose again. Then Peter. Everywhere but at Seth.

"Let's go outside and talk."

He nods, and I walk away without looking at anyone. I
know Rose is cutting me into shreds with her eyes. I don't know
what Seth is thinking or doing or feeling or anything. I
know I'm not coming back to this party, though, and I don't
know why.

We get to the front door and I look back into the room. Just
one glimpse.

And I feel myself shattering.

I sit in the passenger seat of the truck, and Peter drives, and
we haven't said anything since we left the party. This is the

wrong thing for me to do right now, but I just can't stop. I have missed him so much. I want to be stronger than this. I want to throw myself into the new trajectory, but this one isn't over yet. The curtain hasn't closed. I either have to do that now or I have to reopen it for Act II. Or are we in Act III yet?

```
ACT III
SCENE 1
```

```
Peter Comes Back Into My Life.
Past and Present Reunite.
No More Looking Back.
```

What is Rose telling Seth right now?

The truck slows down and we're back. Our spot. Our secret overlook point. Exactly where I knew he would drive us. Below, the ocean is black and endless. The sky is covered in a thick dark cloud, hiding the stars. Everything is dark. Everything.

When we stop, we still don't talk. But we're kissing. We're kissing because that means we don't have to talk. His lips are cold and black and I'm choking in his mouth. But I keep kissing him. Kissing him and crying and kissing him and trying so hard to feel close to him again.

"I miss you, Genesis."

"How is this real? How are you telling me you miss me?"

He doesn't say anything. We cry into each other.

"You're the one who left. *You* are."

I left too though. When did we leave each other? It was definitely before the clinic. There wasn't a moment. It was a gradual seeping sadness that comes so slowly, and eats half of you before you notice. It's easier to blame a moment.

It's easier to kiss instead of talk.

It's easier to overlook.

Can we fix this? Should we?

If there was more light, I'd be able to see if his cheeks were filled up with red-hot blood, or faded into white. If there was more light, I could read his face, read his confusion or sadness or relief or what it is he's feeling, but I can't. And I'm choking on the darkness. The lack of light. The lack of knowing.

"Why did you leave?"

"I told you I would leave you if you went through with it," he says.

This cracks me open, unleashes something wild. "Shut up. Just shut up."

"I did! I told you!"

"But we made the decision together."

"You made the decision, Gen. I agreed to let you decide."

"Then why did you show up in the morning? Why did you take me there? Why?"

"I wanted to be with you. I wanted to. And then I didn't know how to anymore. It's the worst thing I've ever done."

I scream. I scream high up to the moon that doesn't exist tonight. I scream to shut up to shut up to shut up. And then he wraps his arms around me and holds on tight and I say *no* over and over again until they are whispers. He smells so familiar. He knows how to hold me. He knows how to settle all my rage. It's as simple as a quiet hushing into my ear and a strong, solid body that says fall. Fall into me and let me be your support. It's the easiest place to be. And I almost lost it. I almost lost him.

"I couldn't do it. I didn't think I could do it."

I know this is what he said to me. I know he told me everything. I know he stayed with me even when his mother said not to. Even when there was so much to lose.

"I miss you so much, Genesis. I made such a huge mistake. You're my forever girl. You're my forever. I know why you had to do it. I know it was for our forever."

"It was for us. It's not the right time. It's just not."

Everything about his face is turned down. It's the saddest I've ever seen him look.

"I screwed up, Genesis. I'm so sorry."

"Don't do this to me right now."

Then we're kissing again and his mouth is not a black hole. It's softer. Safer. He backs away, straightens, and says, "Were you there with a guy?"

"Peter."

"Were you?"

I tuck my hair behind my ears.

"Yes, I was."

"Genesis, we haven't broken up yet."

"What are you talking about? Of course we've broken up. Or more accurately: You left me. You can't run away like that and then expect me to stay."

"I never wanted to leave you."

"But you did."

"I did."

"What are you saying right now? That you want to be with me?"

"I am with you."

How is he saying everything I wanted him to just three days ago? Did whatever dream liquid we were suspended in at Rose's house pour down the dark New Jersey highway? Did we just spill back into our safe place?

Am I about to wake up and not know where I am?

We sit in heavy silence for what could be light-years, letting everything sink back in. Sink back together.

"I need to get out of here," I say.

"Where can I take you?"

I can't face the party, what I've done to everyone there. So I just say, "Home."

Peter turns the ignition. I rest my head on the cold glass as we pull into the rolling darkness.

I look at the clock.

Midnight.

Now it really is my birthday.

ACT IV
SCENE 1

(This scene takes place in the exam
room at Planned Parenthood. GENESIS
sits on the edge of the examination
table, dressed for the procedure. The
DOULA sits next to her in a chair, the
DOCTOR on a stool in front of her.)

                    DOCTOR
          Do you have any last
          questions before we start
          the procedure?

                    GENESIS
          No. I'm ready.

DOCTOR
(Looking through papers on a clipboard)
You're sure you don't want
any level of sedation?

GENESIS (TO AUDIENCE)
What I want to tell her
is: "I'm sure. I need to
feel this. I need to know
it's real. I need to feel
it leaving. I need to feel
that I'm making a choice
and it's mine." But I just
nod.

(DOULA takes GENESIS's hand. A loud
hammering noise is heard.)

GENESIS
What's that noise?

DOCTOR
That's just the heater,
sweetie. Old building.

GENESIS
Oh.

DOCTOR
Put your feet up in the
stirrups. Then scoot your
bottom down toward me.

(She does.)
>   I need to determine the
>   position of your uterus.
(The hammering starts again. GENESIS
closes her legs.)
>   That's just the heater,
>   sweetie. Try to relax,
>   okay? Now, I'm going to
>   insert two fingers, then
>   press into your abdomen.
(Pause)
>   Are you okay, sweetie?

>   GENESIS (UNDER HER BREATH)
>   Would you quit calling me
>   "sweetie"?

>   DOCTOR
>   What?

>   GENESIS
>   Nothing.

>   DOCTOR
>   This is the speculum. You
>   might feel a cramp as I
>   open up your cervix to get
>   to your uterus.

(GENESIS looks up to the ceiling.)

      GENESIS (TO AUDIENCE)
    What you can't see is
    that there is a poster
    right above my head, in
    my line of vision. A
    tropical beach scene.
    Somewhere for me to be
    other than here.

(DOCTOR administers the local
anesthesia and GENESIS digs her free
hand into the crinkly paper underneath
her. DOULA holds tightly to the other.)

          DOCTOR
    Good job, sweetie. That
    burning sensation is
    normal. It should be over
    in just a second. And then
    you won't feel a thing.
(DOCTOR procures a metal rod.)
    This is to dilate your
    cervix.
(She begins. GENESIS moves her hand to
her stomach.)
    Are you doing okay,
    sweetie?
(DOCTOR pulls her face mask aside.
GENESIS nods.)

Are you sure? Remember you
have to tell me if
anything feels too
uncomfortable.

GENESIS
I'm fine. Is it almost
over?

DOCTOR
Almost.
(DOCTOR inserts plastic tube, and we
hear the buzzing sound of a machine.
GENESIS hums.)
(The machine stops.)
You're all good.
(DOCTOR removes speculum.)

GENESIS
That's it?

DOCTOR
That's it. Leyla will walk
you to the recovery
room. You'll take some
antibiotics, and when you
feel ready, we'll go over
the aftercare instructions
and then you can go.

                    GENESIS
         Okay.

                    DOCTOR
         You did very well,
         Genesis.
(Pause)
         You're probably going to
         feel a lot of things in
         the weeks to come. No
         one has the right to
         criticize what you did
         with your own body. I just
         want you to remember that
         today you made a choice
         that was right for you,
         okay?

                    GENESIS
         I know.

                    DOCTOR
         Good. Now go rest. No
         rush.

                    GENESIS
         Thank you.

                    DOCTOR
         You're welcome. You have
         someone to escort you
         home, right?

                    GENESIS
          Yes. My boyfriend. He's in
          the waiting room.

(Lights fade to blackout.)

NO SWIMMING

The drive back into town is silent. No music. No voices. Just the sound of the world outside the car. We are suspended in the blur of movement around us. I don't know what holds me together. I don't know what keeps me from exploding, but I swear if Peter opens his mouth, if he even looks at me, then I might burst open. I keep my hand on the door handle.

I want to blame this all on Peter, but this moment is mine. This shame I feel for leaving the birthday party Rose planned for me, for leaving the boy who paid so much money to get me there in a cab, for not acknowledging anyone who came over to celebrate with us, that's all mine. Maybe we deserve each other.

Peter is doing that thing with his mouth where he tries not to smile but instead his lips sort of jut out. I used to think it was cute.

I'm in Peter's truck again. My seat. My spot.

My house is dark when we arrive. My mom must be asleep. I wonder if she remembers it's my birthday. I wonder if she'll ever get out of her pool of sadness. She's not expecting me. Rose arranged that too.

Neither of us gets out of the car.

This is the moment where the whole stage is dark and a weak spotlight focuses on these two people who fell in love with each other, who made promises to each other, who don't know which direction to turn, who lost the last pages of their scripts and have to improvise now.

"I didn't want to leave. But I told you I couldn't handle it." He started.

I follow: "Did you really want to have a child with me?"

"No."

"But you do realize that it happened?"

"Yes."

"Did you tell your mom?"

"I did."

I can't believe this. After everything. After all he begged me to keep it secret, he told his mom?

"She forbade me to talk to you ever again."

"She tried that once before."

"I know. But this time she meant it."

"And did you defend me?"

"Genesis, do you know I had to make a hard decision too? Do you know my whole life I've been told this was a mortal sin? That it's murder? It's pretty much the worst thing anyone can do."

"How is that supposed to make me feel?"

"It broke me apart to leave you, but I couldn't stay."

"Where did you go?"

"Home."

"And your mom wondered why you weren't at school? And you told her everything?"

"Yes."

"So she wins."

"You have no idea how hard this has been for me."

"I'm sorry. You knew what you were getting into."

"You always say that, Genesis. You always think no one can handle you and you're the only one who struggles."

"What could you possibly struggle with?"

"I love my family, Gen. You might not agree with everything we do, but they raised me. They *made* me. And you loved me for me. Believe it or not, it's not a competition between you and my mother."

"Peter, I do love you."

"I love you too, Genesis. With all of my heart. I just got scared."

Silence.

"I wish I could watch our whole relationship on instant replay and see where it actually broke down," I finally say.

"I wish that too."

"We can't, though."

"I know."

"I'm sorry I let my family get in the way."

"I did the exact same thing."

Does love have to be so hard? Is it always?

"I wanted this to be everything."

"It was everything."

"I don't know how to be without you."

Our faces are so close together, like we're about to kiss. We used to kiss so perfectly. The perfect, steamy, heart-crushing kiss. I want to believe I've felt true love. That my love for Peter and his love for me was so real it could break through mountains and part seas and all that.

And maybe it did.

Our lips meet. Because they are supposed to. And this is some other kind of good-bye. The kind that means hello to something else.

He walks me to the door because he always did. Because he would never not. I want to keep him here, hold on to him all night. But he's already late. He's already staying longer than he's supposed to.

We enter my house, and I'm struck cold. It's quiet, airless. Like we dove into the deep end, walking through the door. The urge to check on my mom rushes through me. I want to fight this and be in the moment with Peter. I want him to know sometimes it can be about us and not about our families. But it's too quiet. Too cold.

"I need to check on her."

He nods.

And when I open the door to her bedroom and see her on the floor instead of in bed with an empty pill bottle next to her and vomit spilled down her chest, I scream as loud as a person can with a tidal wave crashing down on their head.

The rest weaves together like this:

I can't see because my eyes are full of tears.

I can't talk because my throat is full of glue.

I can't breathe because I don't know if my mother can.

Then SNAP! I'm pumping her chest the way we had to learn

in gym and I'm breathing into her mouth. Peter calls an ambulance, and in those minutes that are actually eternities, I breathe for her, make her heart beat. I'm not letting go.

"Stay here. Stay here. Stay here. Stay."

Where does she want to go?

"Stay here, Mommy. You can't leave me. You can't."

I'm her breath until the sirens take over and the lights and the stretchers and the air pump and the ride through Point Shelley is blurring, zipping, merging, spinning.

When we arrive at the hospital, I have to let them take her. I have to let them work on her. I can't do anything from here. I can't do anything but wait.

And Peter holds on tight while I do.

ACT V
SCENE 1

I wake up with my head on Peter's shoulder. I'm covered with
a thin burgundy blanket. This is a waiting room. It smells like
bleach and something sweet, like strawberry. He wakes up
with me and draws me into his chest. The cold metal armrest
between us keeps our bodies separate.

"Is she . . . ?" How do I finish that sentence?

Dead?

Alive?

Conscious?

Relieved?

Disappointed?

"She's going to be fine, Genesis. She hasn't woken up yet, but there doesn't seem to be brain damage or liver failure or anything like that."

Apparently, the doctors have talked to us. Apparently, I insisted on sleeping here at the hospital, and not calling anyone. Apparently, the doctors have called my mother's parents, and they will be here any moment.

Apparently, this time, once she wakes up, she will not be released.

"Let's go to the cafeteria," Peter says.

I follow him, like it's so easy, like it's the only thing I know how to do. Peter gets us both coffee. He asks if I'm hungry, but I shake my head.

"Table for two by the window?"

Is it okay to laugh right now? Is it okay to smile at the full circle of life? I don't laugh. But I do smile.

"We've done this before."

"The best first date I've ever been on."

"Peter?"

"Yes?"

"Thank you so much. Just . . . thank you."

He doesn't look one hundred years old anymore. He looks like someone I love. Someone who took care of me when I needed it most, and who probably always will. But it's also as if I'm looking at him through smudged glass. An imperfect picture.

"What's happening right now?"

"I don't know."

"I can't do this anymore, Peter."

Six words. Six words that don't sound harsh or cold. Six words that are for both of us.

"I wish I could take back what I did to you."

"It isn't about that."

We can't erase that. But somehow we needed it. Somehow, it propelled us, altered our course, made us see things clearly.

"I'm here for you if you need anything," he says to me.

"I know that."

"Is this it?"

I think maybe we both ask this question at the same time. I think maybe we've helped each other and we've hurt each other and we need each other, but we need to untangle ourselves. I needed him. I survived because of him.

I think about kissing him. The good-bye kiss. The perfect ending. Here.

He leans in, but I put two fingers on his lips. That's it. His eyes sparkle with tears, and he swallows.

"I'm going to be okay," I say.

"I know you are. . . . I just have one question for you."

"Okay."

"Is it bigger than a breadbox?"

A laugh escapes me like a gurgle. Twenty Questions. We hug one more time. For a little bit too long.

Then I watch him walk away.

Our coffee sits untouched, with the last few traces of steam floating over the black liquid.

ACT V
SCENE 2

Back in the waiting room, my sister rushes up and wraps herself around me. We are all arms and tears. Ally is the one
everyone wanted to protect the most. The little girl who didn't
ever know what was going on. The little girl who wouldn't ever
understand. Now, she's not even the same age I was when Dad
died, and she knows so much more than I ever did. I peel her
off me, but keep her hand in mine.

My grandparents are there too. They gesture for me to sit
with them.

My sister lets go of my hand. I sit two seats away from them.

"Are you okay, Genesis?" my grandmother asks.

There we go with that question again. And maybe all that's happened hasn't quite hit me yet. I'm pretty good at the delayed response, I guess. *Are you okay?* Is it okay to be okay when in the past week, this is the inventory:

1. Abortion
2. Breakup
3. Suicide attempt
4. Breakup, part two

And somewhere within all that I met another guy? What universe is this? Where have I landed?

"There was a note, honey," my grandma says. I didn't even think of that.

"Where is it?"

I fight the urge to stand.

"The police have it now."

Police. There were policemen last night. Asking so many questions. Wanting every detail. There weren't any details last night, though. Only instincts.

"What did it say?"

She looks down. Down down down into her lap, and she starts to shake and pull her sweater up on either side of her face. She's fighting something. Fighting something in herself that looks like it's trying to scratch its way out of her, the way she twists and jerks. My grandfather takes her hand with one of his and the other goes around her back. Embracing her until she stops. I hold my tears in my throat. Ally drops down onto the floor and buries her head into my lap.

"I want you to know when and if you do see it, none of this is your fault. None of it."

"What did it say?"

"It's not your fault, Genesis."

Ally wraps her arms around my legs. She looks up at me, chin on my knee with eyes wide open.

"She said that this time you would be ready to take things on. This time you wouldn't need her so much."

This time.

Grandma just said what none of us have said. Ever. What all of us kept in so tight and buried.

This time means there was a last time.

And everyone knew it.

"The first time she went to the hospital, we should have gotten her the help she needed then. You were too young. The responsibility should not have been yours."

Grandma's gray eyes are red, and there is makeup running through the creases in her skin and down the tip of her nose.

"She needed me."

"And you needed us. More. We pushed to get her out of the psych ward. Probably too soon. We let it be something else for your sake."

I want to exit. Not stage right. Not stage left. Just straight through the audience, outside to breathe and let the sunlight hit me and remind me that sometimes you can break from the script. Sometimes you have to. But I need to be here now, in it. To the end.

The script all along has been: not a suicide attempt, not a suicide attempt, not a suicide attempt, just a bad drug reaction. She didn't want to leave us, but still we had to fight to keep her.

"It's our fault. We abandoned her so many times. . . ." She chokes on her words.

Ally is still on the floor. Listening. Waiting.

"Gran," I say.

"So many times. We made so many mistakes."

Some part of my stern grandmother has melted away and all I see is her heart. A giant heart, crying and bleeding in the waiting room.

"When she was pregnant with you, Gen. We could have helped then. Who knows how things would have been different. All around."

I try to swallow, but there is no saliva, only air.

Then I let all those words settle around us.

When the doctor finally comes in, hours later, we're all asleep. Delilah is here now, and Aunt Kayla, and Will's mom, Brenda. We all spring up. We all turn on. Our skin prickles in anticipation.

She's awake.

And she wants to see me.

ACT V
SCENE 3

My mom's heart is beating. I can hear it on the monitor. Her arms are bruised from all the times they've drawn blood. Her body is full of charcoal to absorb the poison. She's breathing on her own. She won't eat food, but she's hooked up to an IV.

I push her hair out of her eyes, and she opens them. When she sees me, I watch her wilt. I've seen movies where people have crawled into bed with someone in the hospital, and that's all I want to do. To press her frail body against mine. To push our heartbeats together. But I don't. I pet her hair and cry, like I'm standing over her coffin.

"Mommy."

"Gen Gen."

"Hi."

She smiles, but it comes out like a frown. I see the pain pulsating in her skin.

She closes her eyes.

When she opens them she says, "I feel him all the time."

My father.

"Mommy."

"I do. And I miss him so much."

"I know. I do too."

She nods, closing her eyes again.

I don't know what she can handle right now. I don't know what I can handle. I want to tell her everything. About where he's taken me recently. As I look at my tiny purple mother, all I really want is for her to be well. I want her to want to breathe and beat and kick. I want her to see me onstage. I want to show her about letting go. I don't ever want us to forget my father, but I want her to feel like it's going to be okay. And somehow I think I've been on a crash course here, and I might be able to help. In a different way this time.

So I just sit with her, and hold her hand, and watch her sleep. When Ally comes in, we both get into the bed with her. There isn't enough room, but no one cares. I bring my attention back to the beep beep beep of her heart.

READ THROUGH ALL AFTERCARE INSTRUCTIONS CAREFULLY

Delilah gives me a ride to the city the next day. I try to cancel the first read-through so I can stay with my mom, but Delilah won't hear of it.

I haven't heard from Seth since I ditched him at the party. He has no way of knowing what's happened to me since I last saw him. I'm eighteen now. All thing's considered, that seems the least exciting. Rose and I have been texting. She wanted to come to the hospital, but I asked her to wait.

Delilah pulls into a bus stop to let me out. Then at the same time, we both say: "Look . . ."

Then we both say:

"I'm sorry. . . ."

Then just I say:

"What are *you* sorry for?"

"I overreacted the other night. Then I didn't let go. Then I . . . wasn't there for you."

She chokes on the last part of that sentence.

"Del, I acted like a complete reckless idiot at that party. You have every right to be upset with me. I know you were worried."

"I don't know, Gen. It just all seems so petty right now, after everything."

"Your feelings are not petty."

"I know that. I just should have reached out. And I should not have missed your birthday."

"I don't even care about that."

"The thing is—and this sounds so ridiculous to say now— but the thing is, I was really excited about something that night. Something I really wanted to tell you. And then we got swept away in your stuff, and you never even asked me how I was."

"I am a total asshole."

"You are not an asshole."

"I act like one a lot."

"That's true."

We both exhale a small laugh.

"Also, just the way you showed up at my dorm, then disappeared. You didn't even leave a note when you left. Or text me. I had no idea what was going on."

"It's seriously been a week."

"I know."

Outside the car window, I notice someone cleaning up a

stoop sale—putting away records and jackets and perfume bottles, and a painting of a flower in a vase.

"So, what is it?"

"What?"

"Your good news. Please tell me." And then add, "I need it."

Her face changes; the clouds part.

"Well, I'm getting a poem published."

"What?! That's so exciting!"

"It's just in the school literary magazine, but I'm only a freshman, so that's cool. But saying it sounds stupid. It definitely was not worth getting so mad at you about."

"It is a big deal. I will want your autograph on my copy, please."

Delilah grins.

"I'm so sorry, Del. I know that we add a lot to your plate. I guess what I really should say is thank you."

There's more to say. But at the same time, some things are better expressed through looks and gestures and touches, and I know by looking at her that we are back on track.

"We will do better this time."

"We will."

"She will."

"She will."

"Love you, cuz."

I hug Delilah and jump out of the car as a bus pulls up behind us. I watch her drive to the next corner and turn left, out of sight. The wind picks up, and reminds me to move.

Now, to the theater. I have to think of this neighborhood not as what took my dad, but as what gave him life. Yes, this is where he would come for weeks at a time, leaving us behind. This is where he would come, and where he would slip. This is where he was when he slipped for the last time. But there was something he needed here, something he reached for.

I soak in the winter sun as I walk. Everything seems quieter. Cabs aren't honking at each other. Construction is done for the evening. Everyone is calm.

Seth and I get to the bottom of the black metal stairway at the same moment. His mouth curves, and then he puts his smile away with his hands in his pockets.

"Hey."

"Hey."

"Happy birthday."

"It was yesterday."

"I know."

Pause. We let the conversation fall into the cold concrete at our feet.

Then he picks it back up. "I've wanted to call you all day, but I also wanted to make sure you had your space to figure things out."

Pause.

"Have you?"

"Have I what?"

"Figured things out."

"Oh, man. Yes? No? Maybe so?"

"I know the feeling."

"But if you mean with that guy who showed up, then the answer is yes. I finally figured that one out."

"I'm glad."

"I'm sorry you got dragged into this."

"Nothing I can't handle."

Instead of making some remark about how he'll never know everything I've been through, or never be able to handle me,

I drop it. I'll never know what he's been through either, unless I ask. And he'll never know unless I share with him.

"Only time will tell," I say instead. My eyes fill up with tears. Accidentally.

We catch each other's eyes, and then he wraps his arms around me, holding me until it stops. Until I can breathe.

"I hope so," he says, releasing me. "Your party kind of sucked, though."

"It sure did." I laugh. Softly. "But maybe it got me here."

"Maybe it did." He pauses and looks up to the sky. The bare blue of it. Then straight at me. "You ready for this?"

"I am."

He touches my hand as we walk up the stairs, but doesn't grab it.

Inside, there's a table set up in the middle of the room where we auditioned. We take seats next to each other and watch silently as the others file in. Toby arrives, and then the beautiful girl Seth did his audition with. The other teenager walks in and smiles at me.

"They're letting me be in the ensemble," she says.

"Right on, that's what I am too," Seth says, and gives her a high five.

When everyone is there, Casper Maguire and Fire Lady, who is actually named Melina, enter together. Melina looks at me with her hard violet eyes, and I still wonder what she has to tell me about the past, but I figure there's time to find out.

"Thank you all for coming," Casper says. His voice is low and smooth. "I don't like to give much of a speech to start this stuff off. We're not going to go around the room and say something cute about ourselves. We're going to jump headfirst into the work. The next four weeks, your hearts and souls belong to this script and these characters. I might not even learn your real names. Are you ready?"

Casper looks directly at me, which sets my face on fire, and maybe the tears are about to creep back up. But I hold tight, and they don't come. And he says, "Are you okay?"

I shouldn't be.

And it doesn't come with any guarantees.

But the answer is finally yes.

EPILOGUE

FOLLOW-UP APPOINTMENT

I fold over myself and let my arms hang loose, swinging them around. As I inhale, I slowly rise up, one vertebrae at a time, with my eyes closed. The rest of the cast bend and stretch and breathe, but we are all silent. We've already warmed up our voices. We've already learned the lines, the blocking, the character dynamics. We've already sweat and bled into this script and now we are ready to present it to the world.

The audience sounds are blocked by a thick velvet curtain. I say my lines in my head. I let the character of Gwendolyn fill up the space inside my skin.

Seth squeezes my hand and whispers, "You've got this."

Then he gives me a short and soft kiss on my cheek.

"Places," the stage manager calls out.

Seth lets go of my hand, and I walk out onto the black stage as the curtain opens.

I'm the first one they will see.

I stand on the stage, looking into the darkness and waiting for the voices in the audience to settle. They are a blur of shadows, but I know who sits out there, and who will wait for me after the curtain call. And I wouldn't have made it here without her. Or any of them.

I take another deep breath.

The lights rise.

ACKNOWLEDGMENTS

The truth is, every single person in my life contributed to the making of this book. This one. This first one. Every person who ever put up with me, listened to me, checked in with me when I went into the cave, took me out, got me drunk, made me laugh, made me cry, danced with me, sang with me, bumped into me, held a door open for me—every one. Because it has really taken my whole life for this to happen, for this to become real.

There are some people who need to be singled out. I am sprinkling stardust and glitter all over the following people forever.

Thank you, first of all, to my most marvelous and particularly ferocious agent, Emily van Beek. The one who took a chance on me and the manuscript before it was ready, and who worked me harder than anyone to find this story, to crack it open. Also, thank you to the magical Estelle Laure. You are brilliant, and so very important to me.

Thank you to my editors, Sarah Dotts Barley and Caroline Bleeke. I am forever in awe of your magic-making. And patience. And extraordinary minds. For being the kind of people who jump around and dance in your offices when you're excited, just like me! Thanks also to Amy Einhorn and the whole FABULOUS team of people at Flatiron Books. Thank you.

I started writing this book at Vermont College of Fine Arts, under the guidance of four amazing advisors who all pushed me in different ways. Coe Booth, who let me run with ghosts and traveling theater troupes and whatever else I needed to as I found my footing. Alan Cumyn, who said that maybe it could be more haunting without the ghosts, and who challenged me to be precise with each word. An Na, who helped me find the heartbeat of this piece, and the romance and excitement. And Martine Leavitt, my rhinestone-hoop-wearing hero, who pushed me to finish, and was a safe place for my heart. Thank you, all.

A very special thank-you to Tim Wynne-Jones, Rita Williams-Garcia, April Lurie, and Matt de la Peña. For being rock stars and friends.

Thank you to the MAGIC IFs. I found these people one winter in Vermont and somehow, they became my family. My writing family. We're a complicated and magical crew, and I want to know you all until the end. Special shout-outs to Jim Hill, Nina Nelson, Amy Maughan, Anne Bowen, and Courtney Gibson. YAM!

And to my MAGIC-al counterpart, Tessa Roehl. What would I do without you? You are my partner in all things shit-talking, wine-drinking, over-texting, lampshade-dance-partying, and navigating this bananas writing journey. Thank you for everything.

My friends. My champions. You got me here. You've stayed with me through it all. Thank you, Anjali Suneja, for all the read-throughs, all the conversations, and all the dreaming. This girl sat and listened to me read the whole book out loud. Every writer needs this friend. Every regular girl needs this friend too. And thank you to Ann Bowman, the other super friend who listened to the whole thing out loud—thank you for that most enlightening brunch and all your support. Thank you to Sarah Romney, who went with me on my first research trip to New Jersey because she is always down for an adventure, and is the best person to spend hours with in a Zipcar.

Thank you to the following friend-warriors, in no particular order! To Mary Meyer—it's show time! To Jessica Hobbs Alvarez, the Rose to my Genesis. To Stephanie Levy, for equal parts serious and silly. To Neftali Haskell, who always said, "Don't take any shit from the army," and so I never did. To Christian Serramalera, who lived with me and my crazy for most of the writing of this book and still wants to be my friend. And to all these people for their inspiring awesomeness: Tania Ryalls, Brittany Romney, Rogelio Ramos, Marissa Johnson, Dawn Mauberret, Kate Springer, Eric Springer, Gregor Goldman, Ralph de la Rosa, Emma Kadar-Penner, Jay Green, Aaron Harris, Lila Rice Marshall, Martin Cartagena, Jessica Marliese Planter, Kate Schlichter, Atty Ferry, Mathew Falkoff, Bertie Pearson, Ben Relf, Ben Cohen, Katie Robbins, Oak Laokwansathitaya, James Rickman. You all have my heart forever.

Jim Moore, you get your own line because you are my sweetheart, and I love you. You make my life better every day just holding my hand.

Thank you to Planned Parenthood, where I've been receiving safe and affordable care since I was sixteen years old. Thank you for EVERYTHING you provide to the community without judgment. I stand with you, always.

Thank you to Barbara Seuling, may you rest in peace. I would not have found my way to VCFA and my tribe without your gentle guidance.

And my family. The blood family. The Pipkin Pirates. My *leetle* brother, Steven, who I swear can read my mind and knows me better than anyone. My super siblings, Jeff Grillo and Koko Pipkin: two halves who make up a whole lot more than that. Jill Pipkin: always interested and always encouraging. Aunt Penny and Uncle Loren, for just being the best. And my parents. I already dedicated this book to them, but I want to give them more thank-yous, more everything. Thank you, Jesse and Peggy Pipkin. I really do owe it all to you, even if you'd tell me I did it myself.

To Grandma Alice and Aunt Pat. Wish you were both here to see this. Miss you and love you both.

Finally, to my readers. All of you. Thank you for picking up this book of mine in a world full of a million distractions. Thank you for loving it, or thank you for hating it. I appreciate the time you spent with my words. This book is for you.

Recommend *Aftercare Instructions* for your next book club!
Reading Group Guide available at:
www.readinggroupgold.com